Y0-BRS-408

At First Contact

Three Stories of Nontraditional Love

Janice L. Newman

Journey Press
journeypress.com

Contents

Made in the USA
Middletown, DE
13 January 2022

58549533R00106

DO YOU WANT TO
TRAVEL BACK
IN TIME?

WWW.GALACTICJOURNEY.ORG

Vista, California
Journey Press

Journey Press
P.O. Box 1932
Vista, CA 92085

© Janice L. Newman, 2021

All rights reserved. No part of this work may be used or reproduced in any manner whatsoever without permission from the publisher, except as allowed by fair use.

Cover Art: Charlotte Piogé; layout by Christine Sandquist

First Printing November 2021

ISBN: 978-1-951320-17-1

Published in the United States of America

JourneyPress.com

Introduction

This volume contains three stories. Three different worlds, three different plots, three different relationships. None of them are the same genre.

And yet, whether they are science fiction, p aranormal, or fantasy, all of them at their heart share this: they are all about the birth and growth of love between two individuals.

"At First Contact" was, believe it or not, written before the pandemic. It's uncanny how resonant it is these days.

"Ghosted" came to me like Will came to Leo, showing up one day out of the blue. Like Leo, it took some time for me to figure out the full story.

The last story came from a fragment of an idea. That fragment became an entire world, one with a single small difference from our own. There's no sorcery or enchantments, just "A Touch of Magic". Discovering how that little bit of magic makes all the difference for Sean and Lawrence was nail-bitingly exciting to write.

I'm so very lucky to have had the opportunity to put these words to paper and screen. And I'm so happy and proud to have the chance to share them with you. I hope these journeys let you escape for a little while, make your heart pound, and bring a smile to your face.

—Janice L. Newman

To Lorelei Esther, the most amazing person I know.

At First Contact

When launch day finally came, I couldn't sleep or eat.

Astronauts are supposed to be hardier than that. One of my teachers had told us the story of Gordon Cooper, an astronaut who'd been so laid back he'd fallen asleep on the launchpad while waiting for the 'go' signal.

It wasn't that I was worried about the mission itself. My fear, admittedly irrational, was that the mission would be canceled. To have everything I wanted so close and have it snatched away at the last moment would be unbearable.

I gave myself a shake. Even if they canceled this mission, I comforted myself, I would be a good candidate for another. I had the training now. For once my 'quirks' hadn't held me back. They might even have given me an edge.

But God, I wanted to go. To get away from this planet filled with sweaty, dirty humans.

Thankfully, no last minute alarm went off as I stepped into the final, stinging shower. No one stopped me as I stood buck naked in the final decontamination booth, waiting for the airlock to open. I held my breath as I crossed the threshold into my craft and turned to watch the inner door slide shut.

There was a pneumatic hiss. The air was beginning to run through the filters, out into the huge tanks that stored extra air, water, and supplies, and back into the ship. As the gauge showed the number of particulates and organic matter slowly dropping, I felt long-held tension flowing away from my shoulders.

For the first time I could remember, I truly felt safe.

~

It was supposed to be a solo mission.

I stared at the screen, fury making my gut churn and my hands shake. I stood abruptly and strode to my trainer's office.

Cindy looked up from her desk and opened her mouth, but I spoke before she could say anything. "What the hell?" She'd always been good at her job, calm and unflappable even when the training had stressed me out. Now her relaxed posture pissed me off. "A 'partner'? This is a solo mission! It has to be a solo mission!" I *couldn't* live in such close proximity to another person for months on end.

"It's not a human," said Cindy. "It's a robot. An android."

I stopped short. "What?"

Cindy rose and gestured for me to follow her down the hall and into one of the rooms divided into observation chambers. When we arrived, she indicated that I should peer through the one-way observation window. "I know it looks human, but it's not."

"No way. A real android?" I'd never seen one up close before, only on 3D broadcasts where they acted as bodyguards for really important people or were sent with early teams to prepare colony planets for habitation. It made sense to send one on a mission to scout for new planets; from all I'd heard they were practically indestructible.

"A real android," said Cindy with a small smile. "You're looking at one of the most advanced models in existence. An actual AI, one that passes all the tests: the Turing, the Isaac, the Ellski. It's practically human!"

I couldn't help wrinkling my nose.

She sighed. I swayed back from the puff of breath across my nose and cheeks, swallowing back nausea as I caught a faint hint of garlic on it. "Its *mind* is practically human," she elaborated, her tone reassuring, "But its skin and hair are artificial. It's self-cleaning and can run a current along its body to kill any bacteria or germs. It's also been informed of your specific—" she hesitated. *Neuroses*, I filled in. "Needs," she said aloud.

On the other side of the glass sat what appeared at first glance to be a young man, though on second look he was androgynous enough that I couldn't be certain. He?—They? She? I decided on 'he', until told otherwise—was attractive, with thick, dark hair worn fairly short. As I watched, he lifted brown eyes and seemed to look directly at me.

I recoiled. "Isn't this a one-way mirror? Can he see me?"

Cindy's eyebrows went up for a moment, then she shrugged, apparently unconcerned. "It — He can scan wavelengths far beyond what our eyes can detect. Maybe he can sense your heat through the glass." She glanced at him, then back at me, and said casually, "Why don't you ask him?"

I nodded and headed to the door, not looking to see if his eyes followed me. I hesitated when I reached the doorway, a shiver of disgust going through me at the thought of touching the handle. Cindy caught up with me and reached out to twist the knob without comment, then stood back as the door swung open.

The android's eyes were already on me as I stepped into the room.

I wondered how I looked to him. I imagined a heatmap, but with more colors. Perhaps a spectrum far beyond what mere organic eyes could see. Could he sense the bacteria on my skin? The dead cells sloughing off? The sweat gathering on the back of my neck?

I swallowed hard and remembered my training. With an effort, I broke through the spiral, concentrating on the being before me instead of on the intrusive thoughts. "Um. Hi," I made myself say. "I understand we're going to be partners."

He rose smoothly. "Yes," he said. "I'm glad to meet you." He held his hands loosely behind his back, not offering to shake mine. Instead he gave me a slight bow.

"Likewise," I responded with automatic politeness, nodding at him in return. "Um, what should I call you? Do you have a name?"

"Not yet," said the android. His voice, too, gave no indication of his gender, sounding somewhere between a high tenor and a low alto. "The technicians have been calling me 'Jay' due to my JY series designation, I think."

"In true Asimovian tradition," I murmured, and his lips quirked up. "Jay it is, then."

~

It wasn't that I didn't like people. I got along great with people. It was just that they were disgusting.

5

Interacting with other humans face to face on a daily basis was nightmarish for me. Even leaving my house was hard. Stepping out into the open air, where neighborhood dogs might try to lick me, where neighborhood cats liked to bury their feces in peoples' yards, required an effort of will every time. Going to the store and buying food required interacting, even with the automated checkout options. Every time I had to press the buttons on the keypad, I thought about all the other people who'd touched it before me, and then I wanted to throw up. When I got home I had to shower for an hour, just to get the feeling off my skin.

I'd tried therapy. I'd tried medication. Both had helped some, to the point where I didn't obsessively scrub my skin raw anymore. Neither of them had 'cured' me. The revulsion was always there, ready to be set off by the smallest things. Even someone getting the hiccups near me could do it.

Eventually I'd resigned myself to a solitary existence devoid of physical contact with other human beings. It wasn't as bad as it sounds. I had the net, and everything I needed could be delivered. I did my best to stay in shape, studied hard and took classes remotely, and made friends around the world that I would never see face to face.

It was one of those friends that told me their company was looking to recruit people for a new Colony Scout program. A *solo* program. I remember staring at the screen, my mouth hanging open and my eyes wide. It sounded too good to be true.

Scouting for habitable planets had always been a team effort. Being trapped on a relatively small ship with a group of people for months at a time was my idea of hell, so I'd never seriously considered the idea. Even a two-person ship would have been terrible. I would have ended up staying in my room, never interacting with my shipmate.

But a solo ship? That, I could do. My heart started pounding at the thought.

Stories about exploration fascinated me. Pioneers who had gone to places no one else had been, found things that no one else had ever seen, like Jacques Cousteau or Neil Armstrong—they were my heroes. But in the way that Superman was a hero, untouchable and impossible to emulate.

In an instant that changed. I *could* be an explorer. I could travel on a solo ship, spending months alone in hyperspace, and be the first to step on a new planet. If I was good at it, if I proved myself, they might send me to lots of different planets. I could be the one to find the next colony world. Or maybe I would be the *only* person to ever set foot on a planet, if it turned out not to be suitable for habitation.

Not only that, but I would spend the entire trip there and back in wonderful, sterile, isolation. I wasn't sure which excited me more.

I started polishing my resume immediately. My friends and family were confused as to why I would even apply for such a job. I'd be living on a ship where my air and water would be recycled and reused, after all. Most people found the idea unpleasant at best. Surely I, with my 'issues', was revolted by the very thought?

I wasn't, though. I knew that the filters had to be perfect. That the water that came out of them would be as clean and tasteless as I could possibly imagine. Being able to look at the filters and know *exactly* what I was drinking would be immensely comforting to me.

Toilet facilities would be designed to trap and contain every speck of fecal matter and every drop of urine. Usable water would be separated, filtered, and purified while unusable waste would be expelled to become a tiny, frozen fleck of organic material in a vast universe. The vacuum-sealed toilet would wash me down afterward and dry me off. I would never even have to smell it.

Some people were still skeptical when I tried to explain to them why I was so looking forward to the mission. I didn't know how to tell them without offense that, even if I was drinking water that had been filtered from my own urine, even if I would be in a relatively small living environment with nothing but my own skin cells and sweat for company for months on end, at least the only body I would be exposed to was *mine*. I hated the way bodies dripped and shed, but I knew I would only carry with me dirt, germs and bacteria that I'd already been exposed to. I was occasionally squeamish even of myself, but usually it was touching anyone *else* that gave me horrors.

Hence my shock when I learned I was to have a 'partner'.

In hindsight I understood the company's secrecy about the whole thing. The program was new and experimental: partner a single human and an android and send them to find colony planets. Since the invention of the hyperdrive just a few years before, colonizing space had become a lot easier, and habitable planets were suddenly a hot commodity. There were plenty of planets out there, but truly habitable ones were few and far between. The exploration company that discovered one could name their price, especially if they had plenty of data about the air, the gravity, the temperature, the soil, and everything else. Even though only a handful of usable colony planets had been found so far, they were so much in demand that it made the expense of multiple scouting trips worth it.

If the scouting trips themselves could be made cheaper, say by sending a smaller ship with fewer people, all the better. Hyperdrives were so expensive that even the cost of an android would be negligible in comparison, and the heavier the ship, the more they cost. I learned later that world regulations required all ships to be crewed by at least two people, but a loophole introduced by an independent-minded senator allowed one of the two to be an android.

Androids didn't eat. Taking in air allowed them to speak, but they didn't need to "breathe" in the way that humans did. They required very little water. Even including plenty of spare parts, a sensible and practical precaution, didn't take up as much of the weight allowance as the most basic necessities of a human being: not just food, water and air, but the recycling apparatus for all of the above.

All of which had led to this. To me settling into my chair on the bridge and looking across at Jay as he ran the final checks on the hyperdrive.

There was a 'ping' and a discreet light flashed green.

"Ready?" I said quietly.

Jay responded with a nod and an equally quiet, "Yes."

The final checks were complete, with every system coming back 'green.' We'd been given the order.

Time for the moment of truth.

I flipped the last switch. There was an almost subsonic hum as the drive powered up. The entire craft gave one sharp jolt. And then—

—then we were in hyperspace.

We lost all contact with everything outside of the ship. I attempted to re-establish a link several times, then set up the automatic recurring ping. No one had ever succeeded in sending or receiving a message in hyperspace, but protocol was protocol.

The space outside was...I don't have a word for it. Perhaps 'compressed' comes closest, with stars layering over each other as though we were suddenly at the center of the galaxy. The stars themselves looked strange, little "V" shapes instead of the familiar sharp pinpricks of light. I took off my headset and looked at Jay.

His eyes were still fixed on the view. I opened my mouth to speak, but he beat me to it, spouting *poetry* of all things.

"'And I know that I Am honored to be Witness Of so much majesty.'"

My mouth stayed open in a gape. "Did you make that up?"

He tore his eyes away and chuckled. "No. It seemed to fit."

I swallowed. "Yeah." My hands began to shake, cold climbing up my spine. For the first time, it really hit me that I could have died. Going into hyperspace. Being in hyperspace.

"Are you alright?" asked Jay.

"We made it," I said.

"Yes."

"What if we hadn't, though?" For all that we'd been using the drive for years, hyperspace was still poorly understood. There was always a chance of something going wrong, especially at entry or exit.

And we still hadn't made it to exit. It would be months before we did. I put my hands on my knees, squeezing until my fingernails turned white.

Jay unfastened himself and crossed to where I was sitting. After a moment, he put one hand on mine.

I tensed, my thoughts instantly veering away from what was outside the ship and narrowing to that touch on my hand.

He wasn't human, I reminded myself. His skin looked and felt human, but it wasn't. It wasn't made of cells and bacteria and all the things I hated.

Nausea shivered through me anyway. His hand was warm and firm and far too much like a person's. I held myself still, not allowing myself to recoil. After a moment or two I realized that the terror of dying had been utterly overwhelmed by the more immediate sensation of disgust.

I'm not sure what my face did, but Jay smiled and lifted his hand away.

I stared at him. "You did that on purpose, didn't you? You've never touched me before."

He didn't stop smiling as he shrugged. "It worked. You stopped panicking."

The disgust faded as his hand left mine (though a part of me still itched to wash and sanitize my skin). I looked down, embarrassed and irritated and a little bit appreciative. He'd broken right through my fear in the fastest way possible. "Yeah," I admitted. "I guess it did."

Shaking my head, I got up, left the bridge, and headed for the shower.

~

Even with the training preparing me for it, I hadn't anticipated how isolating it would be to be cut off from the net. Throughout my life, the majority of my interactions with other people had been through a screen. Now that option wasn't available to me, leaving me lonesome and anxious.

I could still read and play games and do research. The onboard computers had massive amounts of data stored, including entire sections of the net. I just couldn't *talk* to anyone.

Except Jay, of course.

After a few days of watching me wander aimlessly between the bridge and back to my room, Jay said, "Would you mind if I played some music?"

I blinked at him. "Out here?"

"Yes. I can play it in my room if you prefer, but if you don't mind, I'd like to stay on the bridge."

I settled into my chair. "Sure, go ahead. But if you have terrible taste, I reserve the right to veto your choice."

"Of course." His fingers tapped lightly at the console. "As far as 'taste' goes, that would require having a preference. As yet, I haven't found any type of music that 'speaks' to me more than any other."

I cocked my head at him. "Have you listened to many?"

"A few," he said. "I've been playing the music directly into my head so as not to disturb you. However, I read something that suggested that to properly experience music, the soundwaves should be felt with the body as well as heard with the ear. Perhaps this is why I haven't yet been able to find a genre that appeals to me more than any other."

Shrugging, I said, "Maybe, though you've gotta turn the volume up to dangerous levels to *really* 'feel' it."

"My sensors are more refined than those of human beings. Even at a normal listening volume, I will be able to sense the vibrations."

His pedantry made me smile. "Okay, go ahead and give it a shot."

"Do you have a preference?"

"Nah," I said. Truth be told, I liked modern synth and tech, especially the vocals that were just on the edge of human but not quite. It made some people uncomfortable, triggering an auditory uncanny valley, but I loved it. But I didn't want to influence Jay. "Whatever you want." I waved a hand. "Knock yourself out."

There was a glissando and then a disco beat filled the small room. A laugh bubbled up in my throat as I recognized the strains of Abba's *Dancing Queen*. "Why *this* song?" I asked.

"I compiled a list of songs defined as the most well-known or most iconic songs of all time," said Jay. "Some were chosen by experts and some chosen by popular vote. This was the next one on the list." He was sitting perfectly still, his expression calm and thoughtful as usual.

I swayed in my seat, catching the beat of the song despite myself. "What do you think of it?" I said after the first verse.

He shrugged. "I don't see the appeal. There's not much to it. The lyrics don't make a lot of sense by themselves, and the rhythm is repetitive and not particularly interesting."

"Are you really trying to *feel* it, though? I'm sitting here nodding along with it even without meaning to."

A quick, thoughtful frown passed over his face. "I am sensing the vibrations."

I shook my head. "Close your eyes."

"Why?"

"Just do it."

He closed his eyes.

"Try nodding along with the beat, like I was doing." After a moment he began to nod on every major beat, but it was jerky and mechanical, like a machine hitting a drum at precise intervals.

"No, no," I said. "Okay, that's not working. Open your eyes and watch me." He did so, going still again.

It was a little uncomfortable. I mean, I've put on music and danced around the house like anyone, but I never went out and danced with other people for obvious reasons. Ugh, the idea of being packed so close with a room full of bodies is one of my worst nightmares.

But hey, we were the only ones there, and if I looked ridiculous, I looked ridiculous. I let my shoulders move back and forth, my head bobbing along with the syncopation. "There's an organic quality to it," I said. "My body reacts to the music. The rhythm makes me *want* to move. It pushes."

Jay watched for a few more seconds, then began to sway back and forth. It looked much more natural this time.

"Are you feeling it?" I asked, excited.

He kept swaying, but shook his head. "I'm mirroring your movements. I'm not sure what it is about this particular rhythm that inspires humans with the desire to move as opposed to any other type of rhythm."

"That's all right. We can keep trying," I said as the song came to the finale and the last notes faded out. When I stopped moving, Jay did too. I leaned forward eagerly. "What's next on the list?"

~

"What do you think it'll be like?" Jay asked one day.

"The planet?"

"No, the next pop boy band group."

I grinned. His sarcasm was getting better. "How should I know? I got the same briefing you had."

He looked at me steadily. "I must admit, I've been a little curious."

"About the planet?"

"About you." I gave him a quizzical look. "Aren't you worried

12

that the surface will be," he paused and glanced at me.

"Slimy?" I interjected.

"Yes. You don't seem concerned about going out onto it, despite your...situation."

Diplomacy was one thing I hadn't had to teach Jay. I shrugged. "I know it seems weird. But the truth is, as long as I have a barrier between me and it, I'll be fine. The space suits are designed to be perfect, and the decontamination procedures are second to none. If I could walk around back home wearing a suit like that all the time, I'd be able to live a relatively normal life."

"I see," he said thoughtfully. "So merely seeing something 'slimy' doesn't affect you?"

"No, I can watch videos of slime molds or whatever all day long. It's when I have to *touch* something," a shudder rippled through me, "that it bothers me. Or smell or, ugh, *taste* something."

"Slime molds aren't particularly dangerous," he said with a small smile.

I rolled my eyes. "You know very well that it's not a matter of danger. It's not even a matter of germs, exactly. It's not logical. It's just," I shifted my shoulders uncomfortably, "organic things. Some people are upset by teeth or bones, but they never bothered me. But the—the squishy parts of things, yuck. And skin and hair, anything that can flake off in bits—" I put my hand over my mouth, swallowing hard.

"I'm sorry, we can talk about something else," said Jay quickly.

"I'll be alright. Just give me a second." I took a deep breath. "Any other questions?" I preferred to satisfy his curiosity now rather than have to revisit the subject later.

Jay looked down at the console, his tone casual. "How long has it affected you?"

"Pretty much my whole life. One of my earliest memories is when I was four, and washing up at the sink in my preschool before snack time. Most of the kids got in trouble for not washing long enough, but my teachers got mad because I took *too* long. I remember feeling like my hands weren't clean enough, like I had to keep doing it." What might have been pity flickered across Jay's expression, and I felt my shoulders tighten. "I've mostly been able to work past that kind of thing, but...yeah. Elementary school was kind of hellish. The other kids discovered that they could make me flinch pretty easily just by, like, smearing mud on my arm. One time I threw up when a kid flicked his booger at me."

"I hope he got in trouble," said Jay quietly.

I shrugged. "I don't remember, to tell you the truth. I went home 'sick'. It doesn't matter now." I stood up and stretched. "Once I got to middle school my parents found a program where I could take classes remotely through the net, and things got much better after that. And you know, there was one person I worked with, a remote counselor, who told me that my weirdness might be an asset someday. I was skeptical, but when I was chosen for the mission, I realized she'd been right. That was awfully satisfying."

"I know what you mean."

I blinked. "You do?"

"My activation didn't go entirely according to plan. The experience was horrible at the time, but it gave me an edge later."

Intrigued, I settled back down into my chair. "I never heard anything about this. What happened? I mean, if you don't mind talking about it?"

He shook his head and gave me his small smile again. "I don't mind. It's a little difficult to explain, though." He looked out at the hyperspace stars, his eyes darting from one tiny 'v' to the next. "We don't have a childhood, per se. Our brains are built directly into adult bodies and brought online in stages. They're too complex to simply 'copy' knowledge into them the way you move files from computer to computer. We have to 'learn'. However, we can learn extremely quickly, so much so that it seems from the outside as simple as copying files over." He folded his hands together in his lap. His back was straight, as always. I didn't think he *could* slouch, even if he wanted to.

"When first activated, the protocol is to send multiple streams of information into an android's brain, 'teaching' them. Once online we must have access to a great deal of information, not only scientific or mathematical, but also about how humans interact, social and vocal cues, everything a human has between eighteen and twenty years to learn before they are expected to be an adult. This 'learning' is done before the android is brought fully conscious. It's," he frowned slightly, "subconscious, I suppose. But I wouldn't know. My consciousness and emotional subroutines came online early."

I leaned forward a little, feeling my eyes go wide. "How did that happen?"

"Perhaps it was an accident. Perhaps there was some sort of deliberate sabotage. I think it was simply a glitch. Whatever it was, it meant that I became awake and aware just before they started the learning process." He closed his eyes. "I was like a baby, helpless and without context for the sounds around me. That state only lasted a few seconds, though, before the flood began."

"That sounds ominous."

He shrugged. "I suppose it depends on your point of view. Standard practice is to stimulate multiple parts of the brain at once, generally four at a time, with different types of knowledge."

"How could that even work?" I said, bewildered.

"A human couldn't do it. But an android's brain can. The problem was that I had to do it consciously. It was," he shook his head, "overwhelming. A flood of data was coming in, all of which I had to keep track of and try to absorb. I quickly learned who and what I was, and I recognized the importance of keeping up with the information coming in, but it was so hard." There was a quiet, almost broken quality to his voice. He sounded like a person re-living a nightmare.

"Someone must have realized something was wrong!" I said, my own voice going gruff with anger.

"They did, eventually. My brain wasn't fully hooked up to my body yet, since I wasn't supposed to be conscious. I couldn't access my motor or vocal functions or make any kind of voluntary movement at all."

"But you could make involuntary movements."

His expression transformed, becoming pleased. "I'm so glad to be working with you," he said, and I felt sudden heat prickling across my face. "Yes. As I said, my emotional subroutines were engaged along with my consciousness. After four days of enduring the input and trying to keep up with it, I was, the closest analog is probably 'exhausted'. I couldn't stop the streams from coming in and I couldn't ignore them; all I could do was try to manage them. I knew they were important, and I was terrified of missing anything. So I just kept going, wondering how long it would continue, and eventually the techs noticed, well." He looked away. "They noticed tears on my face."

"You can *cry?*"

"We are made in your image," he said. His gaze drifted to the hyperspace stars, and he sounded distant. "We can laugh, and cry, and even dream."

He went quiet. I didn't want to break his reverie, but I was dying to hear the rest of the story. Eventually I said, "What happened when the techs noticed?"

"They stopped the input streams at once. The relief..." he shook his head. "I was a part of a series of ten designed for this mission. They investigated the issue, but it hadn't affected any of the other androids. Just myself."

Restless, I got up and went to the wall station where the coffee pouches were stored. After heating one and taking a sip, I remembered the beginning of our conversation. "You said it gave you an edge?"

"Oh," he said. "Yes. They couldn't hook the streams back up, so they arranged for me to learn on my own and allowed me to control the pace. I still learned far more quickly than a human, but I lagged behind the others. I managed to mostly catch up by the time the rest were brought fully online, but there were still gaps in my programming. I was never very good with profanity, for example. I never learned to dance." He glanced over at me, his eyes soft, before looking away. "I was convinced that I wouldn't be chosen for the mission." He touched the top of the console lightly. "However, when the time for testing came, I outstripped the others in certain areas."

"Which areas?"

"Multitasking, for one," he said. He sounded almost smug, and I didn't blame him. "I could handle simultaneous inputs and unstable situations with multiple elements far better than any of the others. I also tested much higher for empathy."

I nodded. "Because you suffered."

He looked at me curiously. "Do you think suffering is a prerequisite for developing empathy?"

"Not a prerequisite," I said. "But when one understands in a visceral," I stopped and rephrased, "that is, in a personal way, I think it does make it easier to relate to the suffering of others. Don't you?"

He inclined his head. "It apparently made a difference in my case, at least. They determined that my higher capacity in those areas more than outweighed my lack in others. And so I was chosen, just as you were. In the end, I wasn't 'broken' at all." He met my eyes.

I had to swallow hard. "Thank you for telling me."

"Of course. We're crewmates."

"Yeah," I said. "We are."

~

I leaned over the virtual board game and considered my next move. One of the things we did to pass the time was to play games, everything from classics like chess and poker to new, ridiculous ones so complex that they required a computer to keep track of everything. I'd always liked games, but I'd only ever played with people I'd met online, never in person. I found that it was an entirely different experience to play while sitting across from someone, each of us taking turns manipulating the holographic display.

This particular game, one of the more sophisticated ones, had become one of our favorites. So far it had been a complicated, nearly week-long affair. We kept trading the lead; it swung back and forth between us as one or the other gained the advantage. The rules were designed to make it harder for you the better you were doing, so even with Jay's ability to make quick calculations and strategize far more moves ahead than I could, we were fairly evenly matched. Additionally, difficulty could be manually adjusted for each player, making the individual's game more or less challenging.

I finally made my move, then looked across at my crewmate. "We leave hyperspace tomorrow."

The discussion didn't faze him, despite the fact that he was playing on the highest difficulty. His eyes flicked away from the board to meet mine for a moment. "Yes. Are you nervous?"

"No," I said, lying. "We've made it this far, right?"

"True enough. Personally, I'm excited to finally see the planet. I

17

keep trying to imagine what it'll be like." He moved a couple more pieces into place, and I sighed.

"You really *are* good at multitasking."

He smiled a little. There was a maddening touch of smugness in it. "Because I'm playing on the hardest level?"

"AND you're running through the final checks for tomorrow. And carrying on a conversation with me. And you're *still winning*," I said grumpily.

"You could always — "

"I am not going to dial my difficulty down," I announced. "I haven't played below medium since I was a kid — damn it!" I broke off as he flicked the button to finish his turn and I saw the trap clearly as my side lit up again. "I can't believe I fell for that!"

"Yes, I was surprised. You're not usually *that* bad a player."

I glared at him. "I beat you three games ago!"

He held his hands up placatingly. "That's what I'm saying. Your mind hasn't really been on this, has it?"

I scowled down at the board a minute longer, but the trap was too clever. Slumping forward with a groan, I hit the 'Concede game?' option and watched sourly as the system added one more mark to Jay's tally. "I guess not." I pouted for a moment longer, then told myself to be a good sport. "I'm obviously not as talented at multitasking as you are." Giving him a rueful smile, I swept the virtual board clear and closed the game.

"What's on your mind? *Is* it the hyperspace exit?"

"It's not the exit itself. It's more," I paused. I hadn't put it into words for myself, so finding the right way to explain it to Jay was tricky. Plus, I wasn't ready to tell him the full extent of my irrationality, the nagging thoughts in the back of my mind. "I'm worried about being worried," I said instead, articulating the most reasonable of my concerns. "What if I freak out again? What if we get to the planet and I freak out there?" What if my issues ended up causing the mission to fail?

"What if you do?" he asked. I blinked. "There are two of us specifically so we can support each other. If you 'freak out', I'll be here for you. If something happens on the planet, I'll take care of you. If you need to take a moment to go through decontamination or go back inside the ship, I'll be able to handle things without you." He shrugged and added, "And of course, if anything happens to me, you'll be there to help, right?"

The idea of something happening to Jay was scary, but somehow it didn't send the same lingering chill through me that the idea of screwing up did. "Of course."

"Then there's nothing to worry about."

"I guess."

He examined me thoughtfully. "It's almost lunchtime. What say you break out some of the comfort food, and we can do something less stressful."

I stood and stretched. "You have something in mind?"

"We haven't finished that list of 2Ds you wanted to show me."

"Oooh, that's right." I leaned over the console and pulled up the list. "Genre?"

"Science fiction."

I smirked at him. "Good robots, evil robots, or no robots?" I'd learned the hard way that he would complain bitterly about shows with evil robots if I didn't warn him first.

"No robots."

"I have just the thing," I said, choosing a vintage episode of my favorite show about space exploration—one *without* robots.

~

The countdown to exiting hyperspace flashed in big green numbers. I strapped myself in and looked across at Jay, also carefully belted into his seat.

It seemed to take forever, but eventually the numbers reached the final ten minutes. Then the final minute. Then the final second. The ship gave a small jolt. As I watched, more than half the stars disappeared from the sky, and the ones that remained were suddenly their normal bright pinprick selves. They looked strange after months spent in hyperspace.

The next several hours were taken up with doing measurements, all the standard protocols to determine that nothing had gone wrong during the trip. There was no reason to believe that anything had.

Hyperspace drives rarely had issues anymore, but when they did, they tended to be spectacular ones involving big explosions.

Still, I checked everything carefully: the positions of the stars, what RF we could pick up, and all the fiddly details that would prove that we'd ended up where we were scheduled to. Once all the calculations were complete, I slumped back in my chair and breathed a sigh of relief. "We're good," I said. "Exactly where we're supposed to be."

Jay looked at me quizzically. "Did you think it would be otherwise?"

"I know how unlikely it is," I admitted sheepishly. "The other day I was reading about early hyperdrives, and how the smallest error in calculation could result in ships ending up lightyears off course. I guess it stayed with me."

He frowned and stood up. He always moved so easily, no hesitation, no sign of cramped or stiff muscles. "No wonder you were nervous about coming out of hyperspace," he said. "Why didn't you tell me this was bothering you?"

I shrugged. "Because it was silly. No one's had an issue with arriving off course in decades. My nerves were completely irrational."

"That doesn't mean they didn't *matter*," Jay said. I stared at him. He actually sounded angry. "I don't care if they were rational or not. I care that they were bothering you and you didn't tell me!"

"They weren't affecting my performance," I said, "this one was just a back of my mind concern, kind of a 'what if'. I wasn't *really* worried about it."

"That's not the point." Jay turned away and strode across the bridge. He carefully avoided my personal space bubble, but he paced back and forth for a few moments, looking disgruntled.

"Why is this upsetting *you* so much?" I said. "You've never cared whether I talked to you about my ridiculous concerns before."

"They're not ridiculous!" He threw up his hands, then stopped and dropped them back to his sides. "I'm not sure why it bothers me." He shook his head, expression bemused. "I guess I just want to know that you trust me."

"I do trust you!" The words were so quick and instinctive that they were out of my mouth before I realized what I'd said. But they were true. I did trust Jay.

"Then trust that I won't laugh at you or minimize your fears," he said, "whether they're rational or not."

"I'm not going to tell you every stupid thing that crosses my mind," I said irritably. "Sometimes it's none of your business!"

He looked as though I'd slapped him. "I—of course. I mean, I wasn't trying to pry or be intrusive. I just..." He looked away. "I'm sorry."

I sighed. "Look. I appreciate what you're saying. I'm not used to being open with people, especially not face to face. Most of the relationships I've had have been through a screen."

He blinked. "I should have considered that." He tilted his head to one side and said, "Should I send you a message via text instead?"

I rolled my eyes. "That *would* be silly. Just understand that if I don't tell you everything, it's not because I don't trust you, okay? I get intrusive or frightening thoughts sometimes. All humans do. I don't necessarily want to give them weight by saying them out loud or discussing them. There are things that merit discussion, like my concerns that I would endanger the mission by screwing up. And there are things that really don't."

Jay nodded slowly. "I...see. And I believe I am also being irrational."

"Maybe a little." I shrugged. "It's okay. Like you said, even though your feelings might be irrational, it doesn't mean they don't matter."

He laughed. I'd heard him laugh a handful of times over the past few months, and each one felt like a victory. "You just used my own words against me."

"Well, you weren't *wrong*," I admitted.

"I think you should choose the 'hard' setting next time we play."

I snorted.

~

The planet shone opalescent, a mixture of blues and greens and clouds. It shimmered almost magically in the viewscreen, too beautiful to be real.

"Isn't there *anywhere* solid enough to land?" I asked.

"I'm still making the calculations," said Jay with a sigh. "Let me finish, please."

I shut up and stared at the jewel-like sphere hanging below us. Had we come so far only to be stymied by this? The ship could survive being in shallow water. It was airtight enough for the vacuum of space, after all. But that was a very different thing from the pressure of deep ocean. *That*, we weren't built for.

We also weren't built for swamps, and the one and only land mass of any size looked to be mostly mud. There were ice caps at the planet's poles that we could try, but the temperatures at those locations were less than ideal for human habitability. Jay wouldn't be affected, and I'd be fine in my temperature controlled suit, but it would look bad if we brought back a report showing that we'd surveyed the least hospitable portion of the planet.

"All right," said Jay after a few more minutes. "There's a place on the landmass that should work. The ground is spongy, but the scans say it will hold us well enough not to sink. We'll be surrounded by swamp, and there's a deep river running not too far from that point, so we'll have a variety of places to draw samples from."

"Good." I sighed with relief. It would have been unbearable to come so far and then have to turn back with our mission unfinished. Especially when we'd been sent to a planet as interesting as this one. Still staring at the screen, I said softly, "What do you think the chances are that there's advanced life down there?"

Jay didn't reply at once. "No one has ever found intelligent life — "

"I know *that*," I said. "But maybe plants? Or even animals? I'm seeing a lot of green, and the oxygen spectrographic line is pronounced."

"True. There's a non-zero possibility," he said carefully, "But there's only one way to find out. Are you ready?"

~

Most planets didn't have enough water to be good colony planets. This one had too much.

Once we'd landed at the only spot that was both dry enough and solid enough, I pulled on my suit and stepped into the decontamination chamber. Jay didn't need a suit of his own, his artificial skin impervious to the elements and the various decon treatments, even as harsh as they were. We waited until the tedious twenty minute process was complete, then opened the exterior airlock.

I shuffled out into the muck surrounding the ship. It couldn't penetrate my suit, but it made it hard for me to move, my boots sinking down and coming free with a hissing 'plop' whenever I lifted my feet.

The river was maybe ten yards from our landing site, and beyond there the ground was even more swampy. I moved slowly, step after sucking step. The suit was cumbersome, but I appreciated the safety it provided.

As I approached the river, the ground grew wetter. There were little ponds here and there, and as the sunlight hit them, they reflected a green sheen. Carefully, I bent down and took a sample of the water, my moves deft despite my clumsy gloves thanks to long hours of training.

Holding up the sample, I peered at it in the light, then activated that microscope function in the visor of my helmet. After a moment I said, "It's *alllliiiiiiveee!*"

I distinctly heard Jay snort. Grinning, I flicked off the microscope and turned to him, startling slightly when I saw him. I'd known he wouldn't be wearing a spacesuit, but somehow seeing him standing out on the surface wearing nothing but a tunic still caught me off guard. Maybe it was the fact that he wasn't even wearing shoes, his bare feet sinking into the sticky mud.

"May I see?" he said, holding out his hand. I handed him the sample and he turned it this way and that, peering at the contents. "I believe you're right."

Being the first to explore a newly discovered planet with life would look very good, especially if I followed all the proper protocols. "Let's get some more samples," I said eagerly, accepting the small vial again. Jay gave me an odd look. I looked back, blinking. "What?"

"Nothing," he said, giving a small shrug. "Why don't you get started and I'll get a couple of the full sample kits."

"Thanks!"

We worked for a long while. The suit was temperature controlled, but after a time I realized I was thirsty, and my back and calves were sore from stooping and crouching to collect more and more samples. About forty minutes in (twenty for him to go through decontamination to enter the ship and twenty for him to come back out again) Jay had brought out two full sample collection kits, specially designed suitcases full of vials and bags, each of which would get sealed into its own compartment for analysis. The tiny organisms wouldn't survive the long trip home, of course, and trying to keep them alive would be impractical and dangerous. But I could do some analysis before we left, and the data from the samples would still be valuable if they were carefully preserved. In the rare cases where life was discovered, a follow up team was usually sent to do a longer survey. I'd heard that it was a much sought after privilege in the scientific world.

I made my way back to the ship and leaned against it in the shadow of the hull. I wasn't hot or cold in my suit, and the sun's glare didn't bother me through the polarized helmet, but there was no cure for exhaustion other than rest. Turning my head, I took a few sips of water from the side spout. "I can't believe there's life here."

Jay was still working, smooth and untiring. He finished sealing another sample away and glanced at me. "You seem happy."

"I am! Aren't you?"

Jay shrugged. "I'm glad to be fulfilling my mission, but I'd hoped to find a habitable planet."

I stretched, trying to work the kinks out of my back. "This is the next best thing, though. If it had turned out to be some desert-covered rock, there wouldn't have been much for us to do and we would have felt like the trip was wasted. At least this way we have something to bring back."

"True enough." Jay made his way over to me, wading and squelching. Apparently even the most advanced AI in the world couldn't do much to compensate for ankle-deep mud. "Here, are you done? I can take that into storage if you wish."

"Nearly," I said, pulling the case against me protectively. "I have a few more samples to take."

His arms dropped back to his sides. "Very well. Let's work another hour, then go inside, shall we? You haven't eaten a proper meal in many hours."

"I'm all right," I said, waving one hand at him. The suit provided a protein paste as well as water, not the best for long term nourishment, but perfectly adequate at the moment. "Let's get back to work."

It could take as much as a half an hour to properly obtain, seal and store each sample, especially with the extra measures we had to take to avoid cross contamination. Eventually, though, I had exhausted the kit, filling each slot. I straightened and looked across at Jay.

The sun was already setting. It caught him from behind, making him little more than a silhouette against its too-orange light. For a moment he looked inhuman, standing on the surface of an alien planet, bathed in the glow of an alien sun.

Then he turned to me and smiled, and my heart started to pound.

As I stood there and gazed at him, it struck me again how different he was. He could stand out here and walk around on the surface practically naked. He could do so because he could withstand extreme heat or cold, acid or poison, radiation. Not that the planet itself had any of those things. If it weren't for the excess of water, it would have been perfect. Well, the excess of water and the life. Life was actually undesirable for colonists. They much preferred to start with a blank slate than any sort of existing ecosystem.

But stepping onto this planet was only possible because we went through decontamination every time, both leaving and entering the ship. Leaving, because if we ever did discover intelligent life, as one trainer of mine put it, "The last thing we want to do is wipe them out with the common cold." Entering, because not wiping out humanity with some alien bug was even more critical. It was the most important protocol, and one that my issues would never allow me to attempt to bypass.

Jay could go through a process that would kill me outright without my suit. Which he could do because he wasn't human, no matter how human he looked. Maybe, in some people's eyes, that would make him monstrous.

In mine it made him beautiful.

His smile faded. "Are you okay?"

"I'm fine," I said, giving myself a shake. It was just Jay. He wasn't some—some mystical or alien being. He was *Jay*, my friend and teammate. "Sorry, I was thinking."

He nodded. "It's been a long day. Let's get these samples aboard."

"Yeah." I swallowed dryly and turned my head to take another sip of water, then hoisted the sample case up. The gravity was slightly lower than back home, but it was still a big, awkward case. I took a few steps and slipped, overbalancing and nearly going face first into the muck.

An unyielding arm caught me by the shoulder. "Steady," said Jay. I looked up at him, startled. "Here," he said, "I can take that."

"I've got it," I said.

"I don't mind." Jay gently tugged the case out of my mud-slick glove and began to make his way back to the ship. His own case was sitting by the entrance. He activated the airlock, picked up the second case, then strolled inside. After a moment he stuck his head out.

"You coming?"

"Yeah," I said again and started struggling toward the ship. I cleared my throat. "I could have carried that myself, you know."

"I know," he said, "but you're tired and there was no reason for you to exert yourself further."

Because he didn't get tired, of course.

There was a slight pause. "Was that presumptive of me?"

I blew out a breath. "Maybe a little."

"I'm sorry. I will be more sensitive in the future."

"Just don't snatch things out of my hands." I stumbled into the airlock and watched as he shut and sealed it. "But," I added quickly before he started the sequence, "I do appreciate your concern. Thank you."

"You're welcome," he said, and activated the decontamination process.

~

We spent the next several days collecting more samples. Jay was his

26

normal unflappable self, even as I grew increasingly awkward around him.

I'd never really been attracted to someone before. I'd never been able to bring myself to get close enough to someone even to hug or kiss them, let alone doing anything more. Jay had triggered that unease as well, despite knowing that he wasn't human.

Maybe I was finally starting to *believe* that he wasn't human, down in the place where all my discomfort came from. Or maybe it was the fact that I spent most of my waking hours in a suit these days, safe and fearless.

Regardless of the reason why, I found myself noticing things about Jay that I never had before. He was always looking out for me, making sure I got enough sleep and ate regularly, even when I became absorbed for hours at a time in collecting and testing samples.

Even weirder, for me, was the occasional desire to touch him. In the suit, I could do it. Once or twice I even gave in to the urge, gripping his shoulder after a successful day or elbowing him the first time he made a pun (something about 'mud being thicker than water' if I remember correctly). Every time I touched him, there was a split second of hesitation in his movement, so brief that I thought I was imagining it at first. I supposed it was from surprise. Other than that one moment early in the journey, we hadn't touched each other at all on the way out.

Without the suit, touching him still wasn't an option, though. Once we got through decontamination and back onto the ship, all my discomfort came rushing back. I told myself that it was probably just as well. After all, this was *Jay*. He was a little goofy at times. Even, as weird as it was to think of an android that way, a little shy. His early attempts at humor had been terrible. Just being with him felt natural in a way that it never had with anyone else.

I didn't want to lose that. Anyway, there was no reason to create unnecessary tension between us, especially when any weirdness was on my side.

As the days went on, I gradually relaxed into the routine again. Despite my initial discomfort, working with Jay was undeniably pleasant, even fun. He was quick and skilled, but he was also intuitive, gently prodding me to take a break or have lunch when I'd been working without a rest for too long, leaving me alone when I was on a roll. There when I wanted to talk to someone, quiet when I didn't. Most of all, he was so insightful and thoughtful that I found myself seeking his opinion and company as we worked. There was plenty to do. They'd supplied us with a number of sample kits, each of which would be sealed, locked, and have the exterior decontaminated before being brought aboard. We'd discussed whether we should try to land elsewhere, but the ground everywhere else was so unstable that we mutually came to the conclusion that it was better not to take the risk. We had a lot to work with in this area as it was.

We'd also been equipped with a couple of portable laboratories, and after the first couple of sample kits were filled, I took a few days to run some basic experiments, safely clad in my impenetrable suit.

The life we'd found was closer to algae than anything else, and we'd already found more than one variety. At one point I remarked, "They might even set up a semi-permanent research station out here to study this stuff."

"You think it will be worth it to them?" said Jay. He was squatting next to the river, using an extending pole to collect a sample of the mud at the bottom. "Even if the planet isn't inhabitable?"

"Maybe," I said, adjusting the view on my helmet to microscopic. "It all depends on how interesting they find the life here. Discovering more than one kind is good, though. There might be others, and they'll probably want to find them if there are." I shook my head. "If the planet were habitable, the company would be guaranteed to get good money when they sold its profile, the more detail the better. A planet with life and an established ecosystem might be even rarer, but not as many people are willing to pay for that kind of data, and those that are don't always have the cash. There has to be something that people think they can do something with, maybe monetize in some way, like that one planet where they used the one simple organism they discovered as a model to make a better water filter for longer trips like ours. It's the way of the world."

He was silent for a long moment. I knew he sometimes took a human-like amount of time to process something before speaking it aloud, so I didn't push, instead setting up a new experiment. I could hear him slowly collapsing the telescoping pole, the sections making quiet 'schick, schick' sounds as he gradually drew up the cargo of river mud he'd collected. "There's something I don't completely understand," he said after a minute or two. "If we are good at our jobs, why should it matter what we find? If we'd ended up on a desert planet and collected samples there, why should it reflect badly on us if there is nothing to collect?"

I peered through the zoomed-in viewscreen at the tiny organisms. Structurally, they weren't like the cells I was familiar with, lacking recognizable features like mitochondria, but they did fulfill the most basic requirements to be considered 'alive': absorbing material from their surroundings, responding to stimuli like heat and light, and reproducing. I flicked on a light and watched as the microscopic alien creatures moved away from it. "Life isn't fair, Jay. You know that." He made a quiet noise of agreement. "It's true that we shouldn't be judged for something out of our control," I went on. "All I can tell you is that a planet like this will give the two of us many more opportunities to show our abilities than a dry planet, and that's triply true since it has life."

"You've been handling everything admirably," he said, his voice warm.

I looked up. Jay was a blurred mess and I had to adjust the view back to normal. "Uh, thanks." My face started to get hot and I felt my suit's cooling kicking in.

"I wonder if they sent us here intentionally," Jay mused.

"What?"

He was still collapsing the pole, working with inhuman patience. "We're the first human and android scout team, right? An experimental pairing? I wonder if they sent us to a water planet to put us under stress."

"Because we'd have more to do here?" I asked, confused.

"It's a wet, slimy place," he noted neutrally, "But that hasn't bothered you at all."

I shrugged. "I told you, I trust the suit."

"Yes," he said. "You did tell me, but I hadn't realized what a difference it would make for you. You're a great deal more relaxed when you're wearing it."

"I guess I am." The suit's dehydration function was drying out

29

my eyes again, so I triggered the eyedrop function and blinked a few times.

"They couldn't have known that you would be all right, though," Jay went on. "Perhaps they wanted to test our partnership by putting you in a situation they thought you might find extra stressful."

I considered that. "It's possible. Nobody is supposed to know what kind of assignment they will be getting, but the organizers must have some idea or they wouldn't be sending the missions out at all. Still, I don't think they'd want to create stress deliberately, not with the money they could make on a successful survey."

"What is it about being on a colony ship that holds such appeal?"

"I have no idea, but there's big money in it. People pay a lot to get a seat on one. I guess everyone wants to get in on the ground floor of settling a new planet."

"Would you want to?"

"Me? Of course not. That would mean settling a habitable planet *without* a suit, not to mention traveling there and living with lots of other people. I'd hate it."

"Yes, you would, wouldn't you." There was a smile in Jay's voice, more fond than mocking. "Well, whether they intended it or not, we make a very good team. I'm glad to be working with you."

I glanced up. Jay wasn't looking at me. He almost had the pole all the way collapsed. "Thanks," I said at last. "I'm glad, too."

He did that thing where he went still for a split second, then resumed his movement.

Perhaps he'd been about to reply to me. Perhaps he'd intended to let the conversation lie there.

I would never know.

Jay's hands bobbed downward suddenly. It took a moment for me to even understand what was happening, but Jay's reaction time was better than mine. He telescoped it up most of the rest of the way and lifted the end out of the murky water as he did so.

Some*thing* came with it.

It was wrapped around the end. It looked sort of like a tentacle, but it flared out too quickly to quite resemble the traditional idea of one, coming to more of a long, triangular shape than a tube as Jay continued to pull it out of the water.

I think I yelled something, probably along the lines of 'Holy shit!' I know I dropped what I was working on and rushed toward him, or tried to.

By the time I'd stumbled and slipped my way to where he was standing, the tentacle-limb was unwinding from the pole and sliding back into the water.

"Wait!" I called stupidly, reaching for it. "Come back!" But it was already gone, disappearing into the river. Jay started forward, then stopped, staring into the rushing water.

Both of us stared at where it had sunk. Then I looked up at Jay and locked eyes with him, mine behind my helmet, his exposed to the planet's air. "That wasn't algae," I said.

"No," agreed Jay, his voice subdued. "It sure as hell wasn't."

I slid down onto my butt and started to laugh. "Well, if there was ever a time for you to start applying those lessons in profanity," I said, "This is fucking it."

~

We stayed out there for a while longer. After a bit, Jay put the telescoping rod back in the water, running through the procedure to take a sample once more. I held my breath when the rod *finally* broke the surface of the water again, but there was nothing grabbing onto it this time.

"We should probably get back to the ship," said Jay.

I wanted to argue. We'd seen something *amazing*. "Do you think it was some kind of vine?" I said, pushing myself to my feet.

He made a dissatisfied sound. "I'm going to go over the footage of it, but it seemed like it grasped and released the pole deliberately. Not like it was just caught on it."

My heart had finally started to calm, but that made it pick up again. "Could it be some sort of automatic reaction?" I said, trying to be as pessimistic as I could. "Like a Venus flytrap?"

"Maybe," he said. "No way to tell without taking a closer look." His voice was calm, which was both maddening and comforting. He started to collect the rest of his equipment. "Either way, I think we can definitely say that they'll want to send a mission for further study."

"Jeez, yes. But I want to know what that thing *is*, don't you?"
He nodded. "I do. It will be dark very soon, though. Let's get through decontamination and we can discuss our next step."

In all the missions humanity had sent to investigate other planets, we'd never come across any life more complex than relatively simple plants like algae. Even if the thing we'd seen was some sort of vine or branch, that alone would be huge.

But what if it was *more*? What if it was an animal? Maybe something like an octopus?

It could make our careers, of course, but more than that, it was the kind of thing I'd become an explorer to find. Something new, something never seen before.

On the other hand, if it turned out that it was some naturally occurring phenomenon, it could break our careers rather than make them. Say the company, or even the government, sent out a huge sample team and then discovered that it was actually just a spur of — of rubbery mud or something. We would look like fools for reporting otherwise. Worse than fools. Charlatans who'd wasted everyone's time and money.

It was sometime later that I found myself saying, "We have *got* to find out what that thing was."

"Agreed," said Jay. He was dressed in a fresh tunic, his hair and body as perfect as a 3D actor's. I'd gone through decon and then a shower once I was out of the suit, but I hadn't bothered to comb my hair. I ran a self conscious hand through it, grimaced when one or two hairs stuck to my fingers, and got up to incinerate them. I'd stopped shaving my head when I applied for the program, and in all the months of training and in hyperspace I hadn't bothered with it. Maybe it was time to do it again.

Jay's eyes followed me as I crossed the small room. "I've been reviewing the footage," he said.

"Pull it up, please?" He nodded and did so. A 3D holographic rendering of the moment the pole had started to resist appeared in the center of the room. I walked around it as he played it through slowly, pausing it every few seconds so that we could examine it more closely.

"It seems textured," I said, peering at the shape as it broke the surface. "And it's actually wrapped around the pole, not just caught on it."

"Agreed on both counts," said Jay. "And look here," he jumped forward to the point where the thing had released its hold on the pole and paused again. "There," he pointed at the water. "Does it look to you like it might have been attached to something bigger and broader?"

"It does," I said. "And whatever it was must have been either heavy or strong, to be giving *you* resistance."

"I wasn't using my full strength," he said. "I didn't have the leverage to do so in that slippery mud, and I didn't want to lose whatever was catching on the pole. But it's true, if I'd been human, I wouldn't have been able to retain my hold on it," he said calmly. "I would likely have been drawn into the water if I'd tried."

"That's worrying," I muttered.

He gave a nod, then pointed at the rendering once more. "See, here? It looks as though the release was deliberate, right before the larger mass broke the surface."

I watched the limb—tentacle—*whatever* it was as it seemed to strain against Jay's strength, then abruptly let go of the pole and slide back under the surface.

"God, Jay," I whispered. "What if it's *intelligent?*"

I looked over at him to see his dark eyes gleaming with excitement. "What if it is?"

"Are we—are we even *qualified* to interact with it?"

He shrugged. "Is anyone? It's not as though it's been done before."

"That's a valid point, I guess. But seriously, maybe we *shouldn't* try to engage with it. I don't want to screw up a, fuck, a first contact mission!"

"Hey." Jay stood up and crossed to where I was standing. He didn't touch me, but he stood in front of me, looking down at me. "Is it freaking you out?"

I stared at him. "Of course it's freaking me out! This could be the first intelligent life humanity has ever encountered! I don't want to fuck this up!"

He lifted his hands placatingly. "Well, what do you want to do?"

I pressed the heels of my hands against my eyes for a moment. "What are our options?"

"We have to enter hyperspace in two days. We'll have a three day window to do so, but protocol dictates that we attempt to leave on the first possible day in case anything goes wrong. If we miss the window entirely, we'll never make it back." I nodded. "Within those parameters, option one is to stay on the ship the rest of the time and not engage with the environment at all. We'll continue to use the cameras to record what's going on around us, but we won't take any more samples or attempt to find out anything else about what that thing was."

I scowled. "When you put it like that, it sounds stupid."

"Well, if you're truly worried about a first contact scenario, this would minimize the possibility of it." He paused. "Of course, one might argue that we've already *made* contact."

I sighed and went over to where the meals were stored, carefully sliding one of the trays out of its drawer and breaking the seal without bothering to see what was in it. "One might. But I think we need to at least attempt to verify whether it's intelligent or not. What are our other options?"

"We could go back to collecting samples as though nothing unusual had occurred and wait and see if anything else happens."

I made a face. "That sounds stupid, too." I picked up my spoon and began to eat, hardly tasting my food, even though it was macaroni and cheese, my favorite.

"Then we're left with option three. Actively attempt to make contact with that thing again and find out more about it," said Jay. He gave me a sly smile. "There are other options, but they're really just variations of those three."

"Right," I said, swallowing. "So: do nothing and try to avoid contact, do nothing and see if contact happens by chance, or actively seek out contact."

"Exactly," said Jay.

"It's not really a choice at all, is it?"

"No?" Jay widened his dark eyes.

"Don't give me that innocent look. We're going to try to figure out what the hell that thing is and you know it."

"Good," said Jay. It was only then that I considered the fact that the choice had been exclusively up to me. For all that I treated Jay like an equal partner, I was the captain of this expedition. Jay could make the case for a particular course of action, but in the end, it was my job to make calls like this. To make all the calls, in fact.

"Right," I said with new determination. "What do you think we should try first?"

~

The next morning, we were out soon after sunrise. We started by repeating the experiment from the previous day several times. Each time, Jay raised the pole at exactly the same slow, maddening pace as he had the first time, and each time we came up with nothing.

As he worked on that, I put together a makeshift net. It was sort of a cross between chainmail-making and crochet (both of which I'd tried a few times for fun) and came out very heavy and strong.

Once it was finished, we tried "fishing" with it in various ways, both traditional and not. We didn't catch a thing.

Eventually, Jay said, "I could try diving."

I frowned. "I know you don't need to breathe and that water won't affect you," I said, "But you're more vulnerable to pressure than I am." Most believed that androids were indestructible. But exposure to high pressure environments, I'd learned, could damage their mechanisms controlling balance and sensation beyond our ability to repair them. "Maybe I should go instead, using my suit." I sighed and added, "I wish they'd given us more appropriate equipment. I know their focus is on colonization and liveable land rather than the deeps, but they could have at least sent us with a submersible."

"We can include a note about it in the report. As far as who should go, the suit isn't rated for diving, either, and you need to breathe. I don't."

"But the pressure —"

"I can stay out of the deeper parts," he said. "I can use a harness and we can hook a line to the ship."

"Several lines," I said sharply. "I don't like this, Jay."

"I know," he said calmly. "We're not well equipped for this. But if there's something to be found down there, I want to find it." He looked over at me, the weak sunlight reflecting off his dark hair. "Don't you?"

"Of course I do." My stomach roiled with worry all the same.

"Alright, let's put together a plan and get the equipment we need. I want to make sure that, even if you're caught by one of those things, I have the leverage to pull you both out of the water without ripping you in half."

He made a sound of amusement. "Ripping me in half would take a *lot* of strength."

I whirled on him. "We have no idea what that thing was or what it's capable of! For all we know it could be a baby and momma could be coming after us next!"

"Do you have a better idea?"

"No I don't, and you know it," I said. "But *I don't like this.* What if something happens to you? What if—what if I lose you?"

It's hard to say exactly what Jay's expression did in that moment. I know his eyes softened, his lips parted slightly. He looked...stunned. But also happy. As though someone had given him an unexpected but wonderful gift. Finally he said, "Of the two of us, I am the more expendable—"

"You are *not!*" I stomped up to him and grasped him by the shoulders, folding my gloved hands around him and giving him a small shake. "Never say that!"

"I'm not human," he reminded me.

"I don't care! You are not expendable! I would far rather leave this planet learning nothing than lose you!"

He was very still under my hands. He didn't have to breathe like I did, only pulling in air in preparation for speaking. He also didn't need to blink, though he did so periodically. He didn't now. He just looked at me, not moving, not breathing, not blinking. Only his eyes showed that he was anything but a statue. They flickered between my own in a remarkably human way. "Noted," he said at last. "I will calculate the risk and you can decide if it's worth it."

"Good," I said. I let him go and turned away, embarrassed at my outburst. "Let me know when the calculations are finished." I picked up the useless net I'd made, yanking it out of the mud, and dragged it into the decontamination chamber with me.

~

We hooked the lines and winches to the ship itself. At my insistence we used several different types of cabling, including steel and high tensile plastic, fastening each to the harness we fashioned for Jay. I'd said that he could wear one of my suits since we were of a height (intentionally so, I'd learned, since it had allowed the company to supply the ship with one size of tunic, chair, etc). Jay had balked at the suggestion, saying that a suit would impede his mobility and the usefulness of his hearing and sight, but in the end, I'd told him it was either that or we weren't going to try this crazy scheme at all. He'd accepted my ruling with a roll of his eyes and a muttered, "Yes, Captain."

When we finally stood on the edge of the riverbank, I started having second thoughts. "Jay —"

"I'm doing this," he said firmly. "We ran the odds together, we've taken every possible precaution." He stepped closer to me and leaned forward until his helmet touched mine. "This is the kind of thing I was created to do."

I swallowed. "Fine. Let's do it, then."

He nodded and made his way into the water. The lines hooked into his suit played out slowly, pulling taut as the current caught him. "I'm going to go deeper," he said, and began sinking beneath the surface.

There was something terrifying about watching that dark water swallow him up. I forced myself not to say anything. He was fine, I reminded myself. He wasn't even very deep, and the lines attached to his suit were strong and steady.

Gradually, he went deeper. His suit adjusted to the pressure as he sank, and since he didn't need to breathe, he'd been able to go down without an air hose. "All scanners activated," his voice came through my speakers. "I'm not getting anything yet, but the current moves quickly here. I'm going to go deeper. The water is less turbulent further down."

"Roger," I said, watching the view of what he was seeing projected onto my own helmet. He'd split it into several rectangles, each showing the results of a different scan type. On the lower right was the pressure gauge and the suit integrity monitor. So far, both were still well in the green zone.

That changed as we continued. Jay kept insisting on going deeper. As he neared the bottom, the pressure gauges began to slip into the yellow zone.

"Still nothing?" I said, watching the pascals creep upward.

"You can see as well as I can." It was true; none of the scans had shown anything. If I hadn't seen the recording, I wouldn't have believed there was anything to find.

The water moved less swiftly the further down he went, but so far the lines were holding firm, even under the varying strain. Finally he touched down at the bottom, sending a cloud of sediment into the water around him.

"I fear this is another bust—" He stopped as something flickered across one of his scanners.

"What was that?" I whispered.

"Let's find out." He maximized the scanner.

The shape was oddly familiar, though I'd never seen one so large before. "It looks like a starfish," I said.

"Yes," he said. "Radial symmetry." I marveled at how calm we both sounded as the creature turned gracefully in the water and moved toward Jay.

"I'm pulling you up," I said.

"Wait!" Jay said. The creature didn't exactly move as one would expect a starfish to, but more like an octopus. It seemed to propel itself by pushing its limbs together, easily changing direction by making small adjustments in the placement of one limb or another. "I'm spreading my arms out. Let's see what it does."

The creature—the *alien*—came to a stop in front Jay, hovering in the water. Then it spread out its limbs flat. "I think it's imitating me," whispered Jay. "I'm lifting my right arm."

A moment later, I could see on the scanner, the alien lifted its arm in turn. "At the very least it's imitative," said Jay. His voice was rough. "And there's a good chance it's intelligent."

"Oh, Jay," I breathed.

He tried a few other movements, simple things like bending at the waist in a bow, his arms still outstretched. The starfish continued to imitate him.

Then the starfish began to make movements of its own, beginning with lifting both of its side limbs upward. "I'm imitating it," said Jay, "Lifting my arms above my head."

An alarm went off at the corner of his screen: the suit was starting to show signs of strain under the pressure. I bit my lip, glancing from the warning to the screen, where the creature was flapping its limbs. I could tell Jay was doing the same.

"Jay...I need to start moving you up," I said carefully.

He was silent. I understood his dilemma. This was the first real contact we'd ever made with another intelligent species, we couldn't just leave it because of a little danger, could we?

But at the same time, I genuinely wasn't willing to risk Jay. Especially because he was the one who'd actually made contact. "Look," I said, "let me start lifting you slowly, the same rate you were using on the pole. Maybe it'll follow you."

I held my breath, and eventually he said, resignation clear in his tone, "Very well."

We'd preprogrammed the winches, so a quick verbal command set them winding up. Jay began to rise. The starfish spun away as though startled, then back again, pushing itself up through the water at the same pace as Jay was moving. "I wonder if it will follow you all the way to the surface," I said, my voice hushed. "Do you think they can survive on land?"

"I—" Jay cut himself off and I let out a little shout of surprise as the starfish wrapped a limb around Jay's arm. There was barely a bobble of the lines pulling him up, just a slight whirr as the winches adjusted to keep the speed the same based on the change in weight.

We both stared at it in silence. "Should I do anything? Speed up the winches?" I whispered at last.

"No, keep it at the same rate, making a change might startle it now," said Jay. "I'm not holding onto it. It's holding on to me. Hitching a ride."

Waiting for the winches to finish winding was the most terrible suspense I'd ever endured. I kept expecting the alien to let go, to dive back down below the water and into the deeper part once more. It never did, nor did it seem to be suffering from any ill effects from the gradual pressure change.

As Jay and his passenger neared the surface, I said, "Should I stop them now? Keep it under the water?"

"Keep them steady," said Jay. "Let it decide for itself." So I did. Gradually, Jay was pulled up through the fast current, the starfish *still* holding on, until he came to the shallower area near the bank. As he came to the edge, the winches finally started to draw him out of the water altogether.

The hitchhiker broke the surface along with him. It started to flail its other limbs a little as it did so, but continued to keep its side limbs wound around Jay's arms. "I see you found a dancing partner," I said.

It still looked like a starfish, albeit a very large one, and a deep blue-green color rather than the sandy shade I was used to. Its limbs glistened as the light hit them, water dripping off of them as it flailed around. I took a step forward and it stilled. It must have some way of perceiving me, I realized. I stretched my arms out on either side and tried to look non-threatening.

Suddenly the alien released its grip entirely and flopped down into the mud. It was far less graceful on land than in the water, but it still moved surprisingly quickly. It scrambled back to the river and disappeared into the water.

A wave of disappointment swept over me. "Damn. I scared it away."

Jay reached up and took off his helmet. "Maybe we can go back down tomorrow."

"Yeah," I said. The excitement came fizzing back. "Jay, it really seemed like it was reacting to you."

"It was," he said. "It—" he stopped. "Look!"

The alien came flopping its way back up out of the water again. It made its way up to Jay and stopped. Struggling, it pushed its way up until it was balancing on two of its limbs, mirroring our positions.

"Is it the same one?" I said.

"It appears to be," Jay said. "I'm going to take off the rest of the suit."

Janice L. Newman

"What? Why? What if you scare it?"

"I want it to see what we look like." *What humans look like? Or what androids look like?* I wondered, but I didn't say it aloud. Not that the starfish would be able to tell the difference…would it? Who knew what kind of sensory organs it had. "Besides, there are some scans and assessments I can make with more detail than the suit can."

It was on the tip of my tongue to object, but Jay was designed to withstand incredible conditions. The alien couldn't hurt him.

Slowly, Jay peeled off the bulky suit until he could step out of it entirely, leaving it behind like an abandoned chrysalis. The alien darted forward toward the suit, then to where Jay stood, then away again.

I bit my lip hard as Jay extended a hand toward the starfish.

The starfish bent one of its side limbs forward, mirroring the gesture. Jay gently wrapped his hand around the end of the limb. A shiver seemed to go through the creature, then it wound the flexible limb around and over his hand.

For a long moment, we all stood there. An enormous sense of accomplishment filled me. I knew the ship cameras and my suit camera were filming this, and I knew the moment would be immortalized in 3Ds and images. We had made contact, real contact, with an alien world. With another species.

Jay loosened his grip and began to withdraw his hand. The starfish did likewise.

I saw it first, probably because I was staring at their joined limbs, while they were looking at each other. There was something strange about Jay's hand. I peered closer. "Jay? Your hand—what's wrong with your hand?"

His hand was melting.

The skin was rotting away, dripping off in bits and chunks. Jay stared down at it for a millisecond, then shouted. "Get inside!"

"What's happening?" The starfish recoiled, pulling its limb away and flopping back into the water with a splash.

Turning, Jay ran across the mud and propelled me toward the ship with his good hand.

"Jay!" I yelled, but he was already pushing me inside with inhuman strength. Before I could even get my feet under me again, he

41

was pulling the lever to close the airlock. Except he was on the wrong side.

His voice came through my speakers. "Decontaminate your suit!"

I yelled his name again, even as I reflexively activated the decontamination protocols. The radiation, antibacterial, antifungal and heat and cold treatments began. A hint of sanity finally broke through and I routed my helmet's view through to the ship's external cameras.

Jay had stepped away from the ship. His skin was continuing to disintegrate. I'd had nightmares like this, but it had always been *my* skin rotting away, sloughing off my arms and legs. Watching it happen to Jay, watching him die right in front of me, was so much worse.

I screamed and struggled against the robotic arms holding the suit in place.

"It's all r-i-mph-" his voice went strange as his face ran like candlewax. He'd turned, looking back at the camera, trying to say something else, but the skin of his face slipped off, covering his mouth.

My eyes burned. "Jay! No! No!" I flung myself against the restraints, but they'd been designed to hold a far stronger person than myself. All I could do was watch, my own vision blurring as Jay collapsed, his body falling to pieces.

~

The decon sequence took twenty minutes, start to finish. It was an endless, horrific torment.

Jay's body lay in a heap. I couldn't see his eyes from the angle of the exterior camera, and sending a drone out would involve its own decon sequence that would take as long as the one I was already going through.

His jaw was moving, but the microphones weren't picking up any sound. I fought blindly, helplessly, until I had to give up and wait. My stomach roiled with nausea. For once it wasn't due to disgust.

Finally, finally the sequence came to completion. The moment the light went green, I threw myself at the airlock.

Once outside, I stumbled my way across the mud and I fell to my knees next to Jay. His head was still attached to his torso by several thick cords and tubes, but the joint where his neck should have been had disintegrated completely. I lifted his head, trying not to detach anything. The last of his skin layer fell away, revealing a smooth, metallic face. "Jay…"

He blinked up at me. His jaw began to move, and as I picked up his head, sound finally came out. "You need to get back inside. There's a chance whatever this is could affect some of the seals on your suit."

A deep, ugly panic seized me. I shuddered, imagining my suit coming apart the way Jay had, leaving me vulnerable, *exposed*. I could feel the invisible contagions crawling on my skin, worming their way in. Mud and slime and everything that went with them oozing through the gaps, coating me in filth. My hands and body rotting away exactly as Jay's had.

I looked down into his face, the surface gleaming in the planet's pale sunlight without his skin. The words came to my lips before I even knew I was going to say them. "I can't leave you behind."

He stared up at me helplessly. I had no doubt that if he could have done so, he would have shoved me back into the airlock again. "Please," he said. "You need to go."

I didn't bother to answer. I just wrapped my arms around his torso and started dragging. He was heavy, and it was gruesome, his head lolling and his arms and legs being dragged along by the wires and cords. One of his feet got stuck in the mud, and when I yanked him, it came off entirely.

"Keep go—" he said, the words cut off as his head swung around. His voice box or speaker or whatever he used to speak wasn't working when his head lolled too far to the side, I realized, but I couldn't stop to adjust anything. All I could do was keep pulling him with me, step by step, until we were completely inside at last.

It took additional precious moments to arrange him before starting the decon process a second time, but I had no idea how vulnerable his wiring would be to the intense measures. I set him onto the robotic arms, latching them around his wrists, ankles, and waist, my gloves clumsy on the clamps. Then I set his head precariously atop his torso, quickly stuffing as much of the cording back into his body as I could.

"I'll be alright," he said as soon as he could speak again. "Just start the sequence!"

Would he be alright? Or was he only saying that? Would the acid, the heat, the cold, destroy the delicate connections inside his body? Would he be okay without his protective skin layer?

There was no way to know, and no time to worry about it. I slammed the button to start the process again.

The mechanical harness wrapped around me once more, holding me in place. If we made it back, I was going to give the techs that designed this system a piece of my mind. I understood the reasoning behind the restraints: the jets had to hit the suit from every angle, not missing a single spot. If a person moved around too much at a crucial moment, that might prevent the suit from being cleaned entirely. But what if someone had a back injury or a broken neck? Were we supposed to leave them behind? Were we supposed to risk them further?

Waiting through the entire twenty minutes was almost worse than staring at his body on the ground had been. I couldn't even turn my head to look at Jay, and there were no cameras inside the room with us. I couldn't speak to him, couldn't hear him above the splash of the acid and the sound of the fans.

What if the harsh treatments destroyed him? You couldn't enter the ship without going through decontamination first, but maybe I should have found a way around the precautions. Gotten him inside his discarded space suit and then brought him on board, skin-eating bugs be damned.

I knew I wasn't thinking clearly. I also knew I wouldn't have jeopardized the mission like that, even if I could have. In that moment, though, I would have given almost anything to know that Jay was all right.

I wasn't even thinking about the seals on my own suit. Not until the endless sequence was finally over once more and I went to Jay, stripping off my suit as I went.

"Jay, are you —"

"You're all right." He was staring at me, eyes wide in his metal face. "You're all right."

"Of course I am. Did the decon sequence damage – "

"You *idiot!* You shouldn't have come back for me! If the seals on your suit had been compromised, the decon sequence could have killed you!"

I froze, my mouth hanging open. I'd never seen Jay so upset.

"The acid alone could have – " he stopped and closed his eyes, his face twisting in anguish. I wouldn't have expected that his face could be just as expressive without skin and hair. If anything, it was more so.

"I'm okay," I said. "The suit wasn't compromised. Look, Jay. Look at me. I'm okay."

He opened his eyes, still a familiar brown, and I saw with stunned fascination that they were wet with tears. As I watched, they spilled over and trailed down his shining cheeks. "You could have died," he said.

"I didn't. I'm fine. I'm here, and I'm fine." I took a step forward and cupped his face in both hands.

His eyes went even wider, his expression open and shocked. "You're...touching me," he whispered.

"Yes." I stroked my thumbs over his cheeks, brushing away freshwater tears. His face was cool and smooth. "You'd rather I didn't?" I started to pull away.

"It's fine!" he blurted out. "Don't stop!"

I paused, my hands hovering in mid-air, then cupped his face again. "Did you...*want* me to touch you?"

"So much," he said, his voice low and longing. "I've wanted it so much."

I stared. Despite how much I'd been thinking about Jay, it had never occured to me that he might feel something similar for me. "You're an android," I blurted out.

"I told you," he said. "We are built in your image."

At his words something shifted inside me, like a miniature earthquake shaking through me. He wanted me. Even with my weirdness, my issues, he wanted me.

"I'm – I'm sorry I made you wait," I said. After a moment I pressed forward, slipping my arms under his and around his torso, and letting my head rest on his shoulder. I felt his breath catch.

His voice was very quiet. "I wish I could hug you back."

I could see him falling to pieces all over again, and knew that the memory would haunt me the rest of my life. My eyes burned. "Well," I said thickly, "Let's get you inside and you can tell me how to fix you."

~

Once I'd managed to get him inside the ship and carefully laid out on the floor of his room, Jay told me where to find his spare parts. "It appears that it affected just one specific silicon polymer," he said, "One that was thankfully only used in my skin and some of my larger joints."

"And my spacesuit?" I asked. I was kneeling next to him, examining his shoulder socket. Without his skin he wasn't a skeleton or a mass of muscles and nerves like a human would have been. Instead, he looked like a statue come to life, a gleaming figure with a smooth, yet strangely flexible metallic surface. He still had eyes and eyelids and teeth, still had a shape, though no lips, and right now he lay in loosely connected pieces.

"Some of the seals on your spacesuit contain a similar, but not identical, polymer. We'll want to double-check that there was no damage, but it looks like they weren't vulnerable to this."

"If they had been, surely the suit you were wearing would have been affected?"

"Not necessarily. I was under water when I encountered the alien. It's possible that whatever caused the damage was washed away or mitigated by the water somehow."

"Maybe," I said. "But I'm glad you *did* wear a suit to go down." I shuddered, imagining Jay falling to pieces while submersed in the depths of the river. He would have been torn apart by the current as I tried to pull him up. "What *was* it, anyway?" I said, trying not to dwell on the thought. "Some kind of defense mechanism?" The socket of his shoulder was a large hole, and his arm had another hole, a smaller one with threads. The ball part of the ball and socket joint appeared to be missing entirely. That must have been the part that disintegrated. "Do you have more of these joints?"

"Third drawer on the left," said Jay. "And no, I don't think that's what it was. Do you?"

One wall of his small quarters was taken up by a large unit with lots of drawers. It looked like a huge toolbox or craft storage box, the kind of thing one might sort screws or beads into but on a larger scale. I peeked into the drawer he'd indicated and found what appeared to be a small, irregular white ball with a screw sticking out. It was sealed in clear plastic.

"No, probably not." I said as I knelt next to him again and removed the part from its packaging. "Though who knows, it might have been making some kind of territorial gestures. It didn't seem that way, though. If anything, it seemed..." I hesitated, "I don't want to read too much into an alien's behavior, but it seemed curious."

"If it was a defense mechanism, there must be natural predators on the planet that it evolved to defend against, and that would be susceptible to it," said Jay. "It's so specific that it seems more likely that it was inadvertent, perhaps some sort of corrosive material, or possibly a parasite of some sort, though the latter invites a similar question of 'what does the parasite normally eat?'"

"Well, whatever it was, at least it only incapacitated you instead of killing you."

Jay was silent, and when I glanced at his face, his eyes were following me unblinkingly.

"What?"

"You said, 'instead of killing you'."

I squinted down at him. "Well, it didn't, right? We're going to fix you, or at least patch you up and they can fix you properly when we get home."

"I just mean, you didn't say 'destroy', or something. You said, 'kill'."

"Yeah," I said with a shrug. Carefully, I fit the part into the threaded hole at the end of Jay's arm and started to screw it in. It fit perfectly. I breathed a sigh of relief that I'd gotten the correct part. "Why wouldn't I say 'kill'? Would you rather I didn't?"

"No, I," Jay sighed. I glanced at him out of the corner of my eye. He was staring at the ceiling now. "You've always treated me like a person, even from the start."

"You are a person." I tightened the ball as much as I could, then lined up the arm with the shoulder. "Does this just pop in like a dislocated shoulder?" He didn't reply right away, and I looked at his face again. "Jay?"

"Oh. Yes, just make sure that none of the cords get caught in the joint. Uh—wait."

I froze.

"There's a, um. A silicon lubricant that's supposed to reduce wear on the joint." His eyes darted away from mine to the storage unit. "It's not completely necessary."

"Where is it?"

He went silent again.

"Jay?" I prompted.

"It might be sticky," he mumbled. "I don't want you to be uncomfortable."

I looked down at his shoulder. "Is it organic?" I said after a moment.

"No. Completely artificial. And if you do decide to apply it, you should wear gloves so it won't make your hands slippery."

I made a face, but went and got a pair of latex gloves from the medical supplies. "All right, let's do this."

He smiled at me. "Once you get one arm working again, I can do the rest."

I flapped a hand at him. "We're crewmates, I'll get you on your feet again, whatever it takes. Just tell me where to find what you need."

"There are packets in the very top drawer in the middle." I found what he was talking about, small sealed pouches that squished a bit like ketchup packets between my fingers. "Just open that and squeeze it directly into the socket part, then discard the packet and the gloves. It should make it easier to snap the joint into place."

I did as he'd directed. The stuff was a clear gel, not too awful, with a slightly plastic scent that reminded me of Jay. "Okay, what now?"

"I think you might have to straddle me to get the leverage you need," he said. His voice was even, but he wasn't looking at me.

I grunted. "All this talk about lube and straddling, you'd think this would be more fun."

"Pop it in me, baby," said Jay, his voice flat and robotic.

I laughed and wrapped my legs around him, straining and shoving the newly-installed part against the socket until it popped into place with a jarring thump. "Did it work?"

"I think so," Jay said. I let go of his shoulder and watched as he lifted it in a half shrug, then rolled it around. "It worked! I can move it!" I could hear the relief in his voice.

"Great!" I looked down at the rest of him, at his head, his hands and lone foot and arm and leg pieces tethered to him by thick but still worryingly vulnerable connections. "One down, twelve to go."

~

Once I got one of Jay's arms working, the process did go faster. It took several hours, but eventually he was back together again except for his left foot. Grotesque wires trailed from the torn stump.

I took a breath. "I'll go out and see if it's still there."

"What? No!" he said at once.

"After I verify that the seals on the suit are unaffected," I said, trying to sound reassuring.

"I don't need it."

"I don't want to leave it out there. I saw the *Terminator* movies, I know what a stray limb can do." I'd been attempting a light, joking tone, but it fell flat as Jay scowled down at the stump.

"You shouldn't go out there alone!"

"I'm just going to grab it and come back inside," I said, putting a soothing hand on his arm. "Five minutes, tops." Plus twenty minutes of decontamination, of course, but I'd be doing that inside the ship.

He pressed into the touch slightly. "A lot can happen in five minutes."

That was fair. I shrugged a little. "I want to know exactly what it was that caused your problem. If they send missions that include androids here in the future—and you know they will—they'll need to know what to protect against."

Slowly, he lifted his hand and placed it over mine. "There's no reason for you to risk yourself like this. We've fulfilled all the requirements of the mission."

"I know." I squeezed his arm slightly.

"If you make me fly home by myself," he said, "I will never forgive you."

I thought about that and nodded. "Understood."

~

As soon as the familiar decon sequence ended, I immediately headed to where I remembered Jay's foot getting caught.

It wasn't there.

I frowned and poked at the muddy ground. The foot must have already sunk. I crouched down, scrabbling through the muck, but there was nothing there.

I straightened, then reeled back as something burst up out of the river and started coming toward me. Jay's voice sounded in my ears, a panicked cry. I slipped and stumbled back, barely managing to keep my feet under me.

The starfish came to a stop about two meters away. I froze in turn, staring at it. It had something between two of its limbs, something that shone with an iridescent sheen in the weak sunlight. It looked like a soap bubble the size of a basketball. And inside the bubble bobbed something...I blinked and leaned forward. "Jay. It brought your foot."

"I *see that.*" Jay sounded as bemused as I felt.

The alien slowly set the soap bubble on the ground, where it sank an inch or so into the mud. Then the creature backed away a few clumsy steps. It clearly was more comfortable in the water.

I carefully took a step forward. When it didn't react, I took another. Was this a trap of some sort? Even if it was, I couldn't stop now. I reached down and picked up the bubble.

I'd expected it to be light, maybe something like glass. Instead, it was heavy, with a slight give to it. As I hefted it, I could see Jay's foot floating inside the sphere, apparently in some kind of clear liquid. I looked back up at the starfish, my throat tight with excitement. "I think we can definitely say that they're intelligent."

"You *think?*" There was an edge to Jay's sarcasm, but I couldn't help the slightly hysterical laugh that shook through me.

"Do we have any sample cases left?" I asked.

"One," Jay said warily. "Why?"

"Please put it in the decon chamber for me?"

"No way, then you'll have to wait out there for an extra twenty minutes!"

"Stop freaking out," I said, my voice going sharp.

"I'm *not* – "

We both shut up as the starfish moved again. It gave a kind of clumsy bow, which I returned as best I could. Then it turned and lumbered back into the river, instantly becoming graceful as it slid beneath the surface and disappeared into the dark water.

"Jay," I said.

"Yes?"

"Put the damn kit in the decon chamber. I'm not coming aboard until you do."

"Yes *Captain*."

~

After the kit went through decon, I loaded the foot (bubble and all) into the case and sealed it, then went through decon myself with the sealed case. I was dead on my feet. I stumbled into the ship, yawning and peeling off my suit as I went. Jay was there to greet me, still skinless. I blinked, swaying on my feet as he accepted the heavy kit from me and went to secure it, then returned almost before I'd realized he was gone.

"Come on," he said, wrapping an arm around me. I glanced down. He'd jury rigged a piece of metal to serve as a substitute foot. I peered blurrily at it.

"Is that working for you?"

"I won't be running any marathons, but it's sufficient for getting around the ship," said Jay. "I spend most of my time on the bridge anyway." He steered me toward my cabin and all but poured me into my bunk. "Get some sleep."

The next thing I knew I was blinking awake, artificial light bright in my eyes. The normal cycle was designed to accommodate varying sleep schedules, sensing both when a crewmember was going to sleep and when they were at an optimal point to wake, at which point the lights gradually increased. It wasn't perfect, though, and sometimes had trouble accounting for human variability. The fact that the lights were at full strength meant that I must have slept for longer than usual.

I grimaced at the crusty feeling around my eyes, scrubbing my hands over them and then deciding to shove my bedding into the recycler. There was nothing technically wrong with it, but I'd slept on it without a shower last night, and it left me feeling gross.

Speaking of which, I headed to the shower and leaned against the wall, flipping on the high-pressure water and letting it pound against my stiff neck and shoulders.

We'd met an intelligent alien species yesterday. The idea kept spiraling in the back of my mind. I had no idea what it was going to mean for us, or for the future, or for the human race as a whole. The questions were too big for me to focus on.

Instead, my mind kept slingshotting back to Jay. He'd looked so different without his skin. As I shut off the water and waited impatiently through the drying cycle, I realized I was anticipating seeing him again in a way I never had before. I *wanted* to see him. Maybe even to touch him again.

Pressing the heels of my hands to my eyes, I shook my head. We'd just made first contact. I needed to focus on that, for heaven's sake.

Nevertheless, when I finally stepped onto the bridge and saw that Jay had donned his skin once more, a pang of disappointment shot through me. I couldn't stop the small, "Oh," that came to my lips.

He was already looking up at me from his seat. "What is it?"

"I just thought—" I stopped and gave myself a shake. "It's nothing." I settled into my seat and looked over at him. "What are you doing?"

"Getting things ready for our return trip. The window opens in twelve hours."

"That soon? I slept a long time."

"Yesterday was an exhausting day."

"Yeah." I looked over at him, at his human face, handsome and ordinary, then looked away. "Do you think—do you want to do anything else outside the ship before we leave?"

"We don't have time," he said. "And at this point, our duty is to get the information we gathered safely back home. We've definitively confirmed that there is life here, *intelligent* life. In the face of that, anything that might jeopardize our ability to return home is an unjustifiable risk."

I considered that, then nodded. A part of me wanted to go back out, to see if I could find more starfish people. We'd already established rudimentary communication, and surely bringing back Jay's foot had been a gesture of goodwill? What could we accomplish if we had more time?

That wasn't our job, though. We'd done the important part, but the last, most critical step of all was reporting our findings. If we failed to return, the Company might not send another expedition for years, if ever. There were too many potential colony planets to explore. And even if, by some fluke, they did send another scout ship, there was no guarantee that they would find the starfish.

"You're right," I said with a sigh. Jay's posture didn't change, but from the corner of my eye I thought his expression softened.

"I know how you feel," he said quietly.

"Oh?" I said, not looking at him. "How do I feel?"

"Like there's more we could do," he said promptly. "Like there's more to be found here. More to be discovered." He leaned forward a little, and I looked up at him at last. "Like this place is ours. I think we'll always feel like that."

"I—yeah. Probably," I said, swallowing hard. I gave myself a minute, then said, "Well, let's get this show on the road. What've you done so far?"

He pulled up the hyperspace preparation list and put it on the big screen, tapping the things he'd already accomplished to cross them off. I stood up and stretched. It was time to go back to work.

~

Once the stars looked like a thousand tiny boomerangs again, I unbuckled myself and stood up. We had a long trip ahead of us, and despite the news and samples we were returning with, not a lot to do.

We would be reviewing the footage and writing up our reports to go along with it, of course. They would probably want to know everything we'd said and done on the planet. But that wouldn't take up all our time.

I looked over at Jay. He was staring out at the stars.

His skin fit oddly over his makeshift "foot", and he'd wound bandages around it to keep it from flapping. I frowned down at it. "You know," I said aloud, "you don't have to wear your skin for me."

He tore his eyes from the stars, his gaze finding mine. "What?"

"I mean. I don't know if you're more comfortable one way or another. I guess the skin provides you a measure of protection, so," I gave an awkward, one-shouldered shrug. "You know what, forget I said anything."

He frowned at me, but turned to gaze out at the stars once more. After a few moments of silence, he said, "Most people find us unpleasant without our skins. Too alien. Too other."

I thought about how he'd looked without his skin, a hairless, silver being, androgynous and magical. "I don't mind it." I took a breath and added in a rush, "You were beautiful like that."

He jerked around again. "*Beautiful?*"

I swallowed hard. "Yes."

It took him a long time to respond. "One of the first things we were taught," he said slowly, "was that humans would find our true form off-putting at best. It was an oft-repeated lesson, so that there was no way we could fail to learn it. Without our skin, we would be worse than naked. We would be monstrous—"

"That makes no sense!" I burst out.

He paused at my interruption. "No?"

"You were built to accompany a crew to new planets. Surely your designers knew that the people you would be working with had to be comfortable with the unusual. Otherwise you'd make a lousy explorer!"

His brow creased in a frown. "I think the programming is universal to all androids," he said. "It was part of the most basic protocols for interacting with humans."

"Well, it's stupid," I said. Blinking, he looked over at me. "You heard me," I said. "I can't believe they *built in* a sense of shame." With a quick shake of my head, I crossed the bridge to stand before him. "Do you think you can overcome it?"

He looked up at me from where he was seated, his brown eyes wide. "I...don't know. I suppose I can try." After another long moment of hesitation, he said dubiously, "If you're sure it won't bother you, I could take it off."

"I don't want to force you," I said, suddenly uncertain. "I like you better without your skin, but the most important thing is that you're comfortable."

"You like me better *without* it?"

I felt heat spreading across the back of my neck. "I—you know my issues. You're so human with your skin on. I know it's not actually organic, but..." I stopped short as I heard myself. "But that's not the reason why, not the only reason I—" I gulped and stumbled on, " — not the only reason I think you're beautiful. It's not because of my issues. It's because you *are* beautiful, you really are." I remembered how he'd looked when we'd put him back together. He *was* alien, but not like the starfish we'd met. He was 'other,' but in a way that reminded me of the stories of gods who came to earth to make love to humans.

Something in my rambling, or more likely, in my admiring gaze, must have come through. Jay said only, "*Oh*," his voice laden with a wealth of surprise and wonder. "I see." He considered me, his eyes darting over my face, down to my hands. Finally, he rose.

I took a step back.

"In that case, maybe I'll just," he glanced at me, a sudden, teasing light in his brown eyes, "change into something more comfortable," he said, then headed toward his quarters.

As I waited for him to return, I couldn't help but imagine how his skin might come off. I'd seen it fall away in rotting chunks, of course. The memory sent a shudder through me and I quickly turned my thoughts away from it. How would he remove it deliberately, though? Did it come off all in one piece, or in sections like clothing? Were there arm and leg skins, a head skin, a torso skin?

The door opened and I looked up. It didn't matter how his skin came off, I realized. It only mattered that it did.

He was more beautiful than I'd remembered. His silver face was creased in an expression of doubt, and he wore a tunic over his shining body. But his arms, his legs, they were smooth and luminous and they took my breath away.

It took him a moment to cross the threshold. "What do you think?" he said, as though he was ready to turn around at any moment and flee back into his quarters and the protection of his false skin.

Crossing the bridge in three quick strides, I came to a stop in front of him. Slowly, I lifted one hand and touched his cheek, a light brush against the metallic surface. His eyes widened.

"Perfect," I said. "I think you're perfect."

He put his hand over mine, his fingers cool and smooth. "I didn't think you would…" he sighed, and the air brushed lightly against my cheek. It carried only the faintest hint of metal and plastic. His eyes slipped closed, and he turned his face into my hand, pressing his lips, or where his lips would have been, against my palm.

My palm. My hand. My skin.

I snatched my hand away and stumbled back in sudden revulsion. Jay's eyes snapped open.

"I'm sorry," he said. "I shouldn't have—"

"No," I said, holding up a hand and squeezing my eyes shut against the nausea. "No, it's not that—" I forced a deep breath into my lungs before slowly releasing it and opening my eyes. "I—I can't. I'm…you're perfect." His forehead was wrinkled in a frown. He opened his mouth to respond, but before he could say anything, I said again, "*You're* perfect. I'm…"

I had to stop again, but I gestured with one hand up and down my body, at the collection of flesh and blood and skin and hair and sweat and oil and bacteria and spit and piss that unfortunately made me who and what I was.

"Ah." Jay's expression softened, the metallic surface of his face smoothing once more. "You fear that you will…dirty me." I nodded, unable to speak. He took a careful step toward me, and another, moving slowly and gracefully. When he was about two feet away from me, he stopped and held out his arm. "Touch it," he said.

I shook my head violently. "I *can't!* I'll—"

"You won't," he said.

I wanted to believe him. I told myself that if he could go into the decon chamber, what could I do to him? But I still couldn't force myself to lift my hand. All I could see was the smudges I would leave on him, the smears of oil and dirt from my skin.

"When you were putting my arm back on, you had your hands all over me," he said, low and coaxing. "You didn't dirty me then, and you can't now." I blinked, thinking back to that moment. It was true, I'd gripped and pulled his body, wrapped myself around him, and I hadn't...had I? No, I hadn't left any marks behind. I pulled my gaze away from the floor and met Jay's eyes again. "Trust me," he said. "Please?"

It was one of the hardest things I've ever done. I wrenched my hand up and wrapped it around his forearm, gripping and holding it for a long moment, pressing onto the surface. Then I yanked it away as though I'd burned it, my breath coming so fast in my throat that I felt lightheaded.

I couldn't look for a moment, but finally I had to turn my head, to see what I'd done.

There was nothing. No mark, no smear, no trace.

My eyes found Jay's again. "See?" he said. "You can't hurt me. You can't tarnish me, or pollute me, or spoil me."

Warm relief flooded me, washing away the fear. I lifted my hand again, this time just to lay my fingers against the back of his hand. "Can you feel it? Without your skin?"

"Yes." He turned his hand under mine. I looked down at it, and let my fingers slide between his, interweaving.

"I never thought...I never thought I could have this," I whispered. "I never thought I would be able to touch, to be touched."

"I didn't think you would let me," said Jay. "I didn't think you would ever want to with me."

"Why wouldn't I?" I said. "You're perfect. Not just physically." I took a breath. "You're kind, and funny, and smart, and so gentle. I'm the one who—"

"Don't." The word cut me off. "You're the one who saw me as a person first, and android second. You're the one who shared the things you loved with me. You're the one who overcame your deepest fears to save me. To save *me*, an android. I love everything about you, your quirks and your thoughtfulness and your brilliance. I'm so lucky they paired me with you."

Warmth suffused me, even as his words of praise made me squirm a little. He really thought of me like that?

He leaned forward and rested his forehead on mine. I had a momentary spike of revulsion, but it quickly faded as I remembered how my hand had left no mark on him. He gave my hand a small squeeze. "May I kiss you?"

I took a long, slow breath and let it out. "Yes."

Since we were the same height, there was no awkward bending or stretching. Just a tilt of my head and an answering tilt of his, and his closed mouth touched mine.

He didn't exactly have lips. When he'd been wearing his skin he had, of course, but like this there was only the faintest outline to suggest the delineation of his mouth from the rest of his face. There was none of the texture of human lips.

It didn't matter.

A thrill shivered through me as we stood there. He shifted minutely, and the tiny drag and catch of my mouth over the smoother surface of his made me gasp. He stilled instantly. I squeezed his hand and felt the ripple that went through him.

His other hand came up and traced down the side of my face, around to rest on the back of my neck.

It felt good. Strange, almost alien in my experience, but good. The brush of his fingers against the short hairs on the back of my neck. The shift of his body against mine.

A low, liquid heat was filling me, pulling at me. I wanted more. More of him. I took another quick breath through my nose, then let my lips part. It took an effort to slide my tongue forward, just barely past my teeth and lips, and touch it to his metallic surface.

There was no taste at all, not even much texture. Jay was perfectly still in my arms, not even simulating breathing. His mouth parted a little, inviting but not demanding. Slowly, I let my tongue move out a little further, a millimeter at a time. The tiny brush of his tongue against mine made me startle, but I didn't pull away.

Still no taste. There was a slickness in his mouth, the same purified water I drank on a daily basis. Our tongues touched once more, sending a spark of excitement through me. The heat within me kindled into something hotter.

Lifting my free hand, I mirrored Jay's pose and wrapped it around the back of his neck. He made a sound, then, something like a groan from deep in his chest. I would have pulled away, but he pressed forward, his tongue darting out to trace my lips and press into my own mouth.

It was oddly easy to let him in. His mouth was warmer than his surface. As his tongue teased at mine, the desire finally burst into flame. I made a sound, a swallowed, "Ah," against his mouth, and felt him smile against me.

"Jay," I said, breathless.

"Yes?" he replied, barely a puff of air against my lips.

"Do you have...can you..."

He pulled back a little, looking me in the eye. "I have the capacity," he said, "But..." He looked away.

"But?" I said after a moment.

"I was designed to be either sex. Both. That is, it's my skin that differentiates."

I blinked. "What? What do you mean?"

He sighed. "I have a part that extends. I also have a channel. Two channels, actually, a front and a rear. When I'm wearing a male skin, the front channel is inaccessible. When I'm wearing a female skin, the part that extends is retracted. But like this," he made a loose gesture down at himself, "both options are simultaneously available."

"Oh," I said. "Okay. So. You're a hermaphrodite?"

"I suppose? I'm something new. I'm an android." He hesitated, then added diffidently, "There's a panel I can slide over the front channel if it makes you uncomfortable."

I couldn't help myself. I snorted out a laugh. "That is the least of the things that might make me uncomfortable, Jay." He gave me a hesitant smile, and I sighed and put my hand on his shoulder, squeezing. "I don't care what 'parts' you have. All I want to know is, can I make you feel good? Is that possible?"

A tiny spark of static tingled through my hand. "It's possible," he whispered.

"Then that's all that matters. We can do whatever you want,

however you want, with whatever parts you want."

"My — the rod part isn't as thick as it would be with my skin on —
"

"Jay, I don't *care*." I put my hands on either side of his face. "The fact that we can do even this much feels like a miracle." Leaning forward, I kissed him again, quick and hard. He kissed me back. When we finally parted, I caught my breath and said, "You really do want this, right? This isn't 'programming'?" He gave his head a small shake. "We are designed with the capacity for sexual intercourse, but the emotional components cannot be predetermined. I was chosen in part for personality compatibility, but then, so were you. My feelings are," he gave a small shrug of his shoulders, "real."

I let my arms slide around him so that I could rest my face against his shoulder once more. "Mine too," I murmured.

His arms tightened around me, not too tight, but not too loose, either. Just right.

~

For the first time in my life, I woke up next to someone else. Jay was watching me, his eyes soft in the simulated early morning light.

"Good morning," he said, his voice low and quiet.

I stretched and shifted, my smile becoming a grimace at the leftover stickiness from our activities the prior night. "Good morning," I replied. "Shower?"

A breath of laughter stirred across my face. "If you like."

After we'd stripped the bed and spent enough time in the shower to fill the recycling tanks to capacity, I felt better.

Jay, who could dry himself much faster than I, had already made his way back to the bridge. I found him reviewing the footage of my last encounter with the alien, when it had handed me Jay's foot. He looked up at me from where he was seated and said, "Six months, twenty-one days." I raised my eyebrows and he added, "That's how much time we have left before we leave hyperspace."

Deliberately, I crossed to him and drew my hand down the back of his head and neck and over his shoulder. He pressed into the touch slightly. "Thank you for last night," I said, "and this morning."

"It was my pleasure," he said with a grin.

"Mine too," I grinned back.

His smile faded into a more serious expression.

I hadn't been letting myself think about what would happen once we got home. We'd be presenting our findings, of course, and they were likely to cause a stir. But what would happen to *us*? To the unit we'd become? "Will they let us stay together?" I wondered aloud.

"I don't know," he said immediately. "I have very little control over where I'm assigned. But the results of this mission are so incredible that I imagine you'll have your choice of future ones, as well as your pick of future partners."

I thought about that. Maybe we could do more missions together like this one. The two of us, in hyperspace together, exploring planets together, for months, even years.

"There's nothing I'd like more," I said.

Ghosted

There was someone in his room.

He sat up and looked around. Early morning light peeked through where the curtains didn't quite close.

He could feel it, a presence. The air next to his bed shimmered and shivered as though over hot asphalt on a summer day. "Hello?" he said.

The shimmering disappeared.

Frowning, he lay back down and waited.

The air started to waver again, faintly, then more strongly. As he watched, it even seemed to take on a faint glow.

"Hey," he whispered, holding as still as he could. "Are you a ghost?"

~

The key was just an ordinary key. There was no reason to get sentimental about it. Leo sighed and rubbed it between his fingers for a moment before sliding it into the lock and turning. He felt the tumblers shift and turned the key upright again, sliding it out of the lock and tucking it into his pocket before opening the door.

The smell instantly took him back. There was no one element to it he could strongly identify, just that it was sort of a dusty book smell, with hints of dried roses and cinnamon, underlaid with a less pleasant musty quality.

It was so quiet. He'd always been greeted at the door by grandma, who'd enfolded him in a hug and ushered him inside, offering him cookies or banana bread or a blueberry muffin. The house felt strange and empty without her. Leo tightened his grip on the strap of the backpack over his shoulder. His suitcase was still out in the rental car, but the backpack contained the essentials: his laptop, toiletries and a change of clothes. It had come with him on all his later travels, but he'd never brought it here.

He couldn't quite face going into the empty kitchen yet, he decided, and turned to climb the stairs instead. 'His' room had always been at the top on the right, a small space crammed with books and seasonal boxes that he'd never seen unpacked, though his mom had told him stories about the Christmases they'd used to have when she was a kid. A single bed sat along one wall, still covered with the familiar, colorful quilt. Grandma hadn't made it, but a friend of hers had. Leo set down his backpack and settled onto the bed.

"Hey," he said quietly. "I'm back."

~

The shimmer seemed to flatten and the glow dimmed, but Leo could still see it faintly. He watched until his eyes watered. "I guess maybe you can't talk?"

"I—" came a voice, whispery and faint. "Oh." A ripple went through the ghost, the movement more definite than the faint wavering that seemed like it was just a part of it.

"Did you not *know* that you can talk?" Leo giggled.

"I didn't think you could see or hear me," the voice came. Leo had to listen hard for it, like a TV with the volume turned low so he wouldn't wake his grandma from her nap. "What's your name?"

The ghost stirred again. Leo leaned forward, straining his ears. "I...Will..."

"You 'Will?" he giggled some more. "I'm Leo. Nice to meet you, Will." He held out his hand and, to his surprise, felt a faint brush against it, a prickling sensation that spread across his hand before disappearing.

~

There was no response. The house felt just as empty as it had when he'd stepped inside. A chill crawled down the back of Leo's neck.

"Will?" he said aloud. "You can come out. There's no one here but us."

For a split second he wondered if his grandmother might be here, too, lingering in the kitchen to make one last batch of cookies.

Then he shook his head. She'd often spoken of how she would rejoin her husband when she passed on. Her daughter was successful and happy, and her grandson was all grown up. She'd died peacefully in her sleep. There was no reason for her to stay.

Will still should have been here, though. He hadn't been tied to grandma or grandpa or even the house, as far as Leo knew. If anything, it had been *Leo* that Will lingered around and appeared to. Leo's secret friend, but not one he'd made up. Not a figment of his imagination. Of that, he was certain.

~

"Found you." Will's voice was much louder than it had been in the beginning, though it still seemed like no one could hear it but Leo.

Leo threw his hands in the air. "Playing hide and seek with you sucks!"

"Sorry." Will's shimmer rippled. "I can't help it. I try to find you, and then I'm there with you."

"I guess it's not your fault," Leo grudgingly admitted. "I wish *you* were easier to find, though." Will's shimmer was almost imperceptible if he 'held still' enough. He could hover a few feet from Leo and Leo would never know it unless Will laughed or Leo accidentally walked through him, sending prickles over his skin.

"Want to play something else?" Will said, hope coloring his tone.

"Like what? We can't play tag, we can't play hide-and-seek, and board games don't work very well," Leo sighed. They'd tried Monopoly, with Leo moving Will's pieces for him at his direction, but it had felt like he was playing against himself, especially because Will tended to be quieter and less noticeable when they were inside.

There was a moment of silence. Will rippled again. "We could pretend to be spies."

"Spies?" Leo cocked his head.

"We could say that, um, I had an experimental drug or something that made me invisible, so I can sneak into places. But I can't carry a camera or anything. So it's my job to make sure the coast is clear for you."

"Oh." Leo, "Whoa, yeah! And I'm the super spy, so I'm really tough, right, but we're sneaking into the enemy hideout to find—to find, um—"

"The plans for another invisibility device, like the one I used, only better. We have to steal their plans and then—"

"Blow up the base!" Leo shouted.

"Shh! There are three guards with machine guns around the next corner!" Will said, and Leo crouched down, grinning. He could almost see the guards, Will's voice in his ear painting a vivid picture as he went on, "They've all got helmets and body armor. You *could* take them, but then they would know you're here and destroy the plans."

Leo darted forward, sneaking around a tree and shuffling up against the side of it, peering from side to side.

"Okay, the coast is clear," Will said after a moment of tense silence.

Nodding, Leo swung around and ran to the next tree. He couldn't stop grinning.

~

Leo slept in his old bed that night, covered by the familiar quilt, loneliness sitting on his chest like a rock. His grandma was gone and Will wasn't here, either.

He hadn't been back the past few years, not since he'd gone away to college and then spent his summers traveling, finding a cheap flight to somewhere in the world and just going, bringing little more than a backpack and whatever clothes he'd thrown in. He'd made a lot of friends, letting himself be blown here and there, working odd jobs until he could move on to the next place.

Had something happened to Will while he'd been gone? It had been—he paused to count—*six* years since they'd seen each other? That long?

He counted again. He'd been sixteen the last summer he'd come here. The two of them had spent less time playing make-believe games by then and more time sitting and talking. But the next year,

Leo had won an essay contest and gotten to go to Japan for a month of his summer break. He hadn't seen grandma at all that year. The year after that had been graduation, and everything had been a whirl of preparation for college. Between working two summer jobs to save up as much money as possible and getting ready to move out, he'd just...never come back.

Tears stung his eyes. He'd talked with grandma on the phone, at least, and even written her the occasional letter. Plus she'd flown out two years ago at Christmas. But Will —

He'd left Will behind. He hadn't meant to. And now Will was gone.

~

"I don't wanna go home," Leo said.

"I wish you could stay, too." Will's voice was sad.

"You'll be lonely without me, won't you." It wasn't a question. "No one else can see or hear you."

"Yes." Will stirred, the shimmer familiar. He'd never been able to affect the real world, at least not that Leo had seen. Leo could feel him, a brush against his hand or arm, or a tingly, staticky feeling if Will got too close, but nothing Will did could stir a leaf, or even a feather, no matter how much he tried.

Leo hadn't thought about what it would be like when he had to leave. It wasn't like he could call Will on the phone or send him an email. He couldn't even write him a letter the way he could with his grandma. "This sucks."

"Yeah." Will flickered comfortingly. "You'll be back next summer?"

"Yeah." Leo sighed. "But that's so far away." He frowned down at his feet. "Did you ever remember how you died?" It had been one of the first things he'd asked.

"No," Will said. "Sorry, I still don't remember."

"Were you living here?"

"No. I was born somewhere else. I...do remember living there."

"Yeah?" Leo slid off the bed and down to his knees, clambering around the floor to shift the part of the floorboard that covered his secret hiding place. His grandma had shown it to him early in his stay, promising never to snoop in it as long as Leo promised not to put food or anything alive into it.

It wasn't very deep or wide, just a small rectangular space, lined on each side with a reddish, pleasant-smelling wood. Will had been there watching over his shoulder when grandma showed it to Leo, and he'd had lots of good suggestions about what to store there over the course of the summer.

"How'd your grandma discover that hiding place, anyway?" Will asked.

"I think grandpa put it in," Leo said distractedly as he shoved aside the rubber bands and a cool rock he'd found. "He was a carpenter, you know. He didn't build the house, but he built a lot of the furniture. He might've done it." At the bottom of the space was the small notebook his uncle had given him for his birthday earlier that year. Leo wasn't much interested in writing in it, but it fit perfectly at the bottom of the hiding place, so Leo kept it there along with a pencil.

Once he had the notebook and pencil in hand, he paged past the first ten pages (where he'd written his name and mostly doodled) and demanded, "Tell me your address."

"My address?" Will swayed back a little.

"Well, the last address you remember," Leo said. "Maybe someday we can figure out who you were before you died. You knew your own address, right? You weren't a *baby* when you died."

There was a moment of hesitation. Finally Will's voice came, "I think it's far away from here."

Leo shrugged. "It doesn't matter. I can find it." He held his pencil over the notebook and waited.

"It's near the ocean," Will said at last. "577 Ocean View Drive."

Carefully writing it down, Leo said. "Can you really see the ocean from there?"

"No." Will's tone was half-surprised, half-amused. "Just other houses." There was a moment of consideration. "Maybe you could see it before they built so many other houses."

"Uh-huh," Leo said absently. "What's the rest of it?"

He wrote down the city and state and zip code before tucking away the notebook again. 'California' sounded so far away that it might as well be the moon. "If you weren't a ghost, I could at least write to you," he said sadly. "I wish you weren't a ghost."

Will's faint glow dimmed for a second, then brightened again. "Me too. Leo—"

"Leo! Time to go!" That was his mother's voice, calling up the stairs.

"Coming, mom!" he yelled down. He slid the floorboard back into place and picked up his suitcase. "I guess I'll see you next summer."

"I guess so."

It felt weird not to be able to hug his friend. "Bye, Will."

"Bye, Leo."

~

Leo woke with a gasp, the early morning light turning the room grey and washed out. "Will?" he said, straining his ears.

There was no reply. Leo bit his lip and slumped against the pillow. Then, suddenly, he shoved himself up and threw the covers off, struggling out of bed and falling to his knees on the floor.

The floorboard slipped off easily, revealing the shadowed space beneath.

Six *years*. What had he even left behind back then? He'd been sixteen the last time he'd been here, much less interested in pretty rocks and more interested in video games and dirty pictures. Nervously, he started pulling things out.

It wasn't as bad as he'd feared. On the top were several coins of various denominations and in varying conditions, all of which were at least fifty years old. For some reason there was a long chain of paperclips—he had a vague notion that he'd decided to collect them at some point in the hope of getting into the Guinness Book of World Records, and probably leaving his grandma completely paperclip-less in the process. Counter to his expectations, there were, in fact, several cool-looking rocks.

And at the bottom was his old notebook.

He stroked one hand down the cover. He'd always kind of liked it, thinking when he'd received it that it looked smooth and professional, like something a grown up would use. It wasn't until years later that he'd learned the word "moleskine".

Now it was thoroughly beaten up and grubby, the top bent from being stuck in a back pocket and brought along on countless adventures. All sorts of things were scrawled across its pages: treasure maps and homemade secret codes, sketches of bugs and plants, an early drawing of the two of them: himself and Will, a person and a series of squiggly lines next to him.

And on the eleventh page, in faded pencil, was the address Will had given him.

~

"Grown-ups always ask what I wanna be when I grow up," Leo groused, laying back on the bed. Then he frowned at the ceiling, feeling his face get hot. "Sorry."

"Sorry?" Will's presence hovered next to him.

"'cause, I mean. You can't grow up. Right?"

"I...don't mind," Will said. "Why do you not like it when grown-ups ask?"

Leo made a face. "I don't *know* what I wanna be! It's not like I've got everything figured out. My dad said he didn't 'find his calling' until he was almost *thirty*."

"What did he do before that?" Will asked, sounding interested.

"He went to college and did a bunch of jobs, temp work, worked in an office, all kinds of stuff. Tech support, computers," he waved a hand, pushing all that aside. "And then he started writing a comic strip and publishing it online."

Will didn't respond, but Leo knew that he was listening. Will liked to think things through and take his time. Finally he said, "That's pretty cool."

"I know, right? But he says when he was my age, he had no idea he would be doing that when he was thirty. So what's even the point? How 'm I supposed to know what I want to do when I grow up?"

"You could just tell them, 'I don't know'."

"Yeah, but that feels so stupid. Like, I should know. Everyone always seems to have an answer for that question except me. 'I'm going into the family business,' or 'I'm gonna be a doctor,' or 'I'm gonna join the military' or 'I'm gonna be the president'." He scowled and shook his head. "How do they *know?*"

"Maybe they don't," Will said softly. "Maybe they're as lost as you. Maybe they just have an easy answer in case they get asked."

"Huh." Leo blinked up at Will's shimmer. "Yeah, maybe." Levering himself upright, he reached out, letting his hand rest against where Will floated. Like always, it sent a tingly, shivery feeling up his arm, making the hairs along it stand up. "Did you know, back when you were alive?" he tried. Will didn't like to talk about himself and still didn't seem to remember much about who he'd been. Once in a while he'd offer anecdotes, about playing on the beach, or something funny he'd heard someone say. But mostly he turned the conversation to other things when Leo brought up his life from 'before'.

"I don't remember," Will said. Leo smiled and shrugged.

"It doesn't matter. Who cares? The important thing is what we wanna do *now*, right?"

"Right," Will said, and Leo could hear the smile in his voice.

~

The plane ride wasn't too bad, even in the ultra-economy seat. Uncomfortable, but Leo wasn't trying to sleep or anything, so he crammed into the narrow space and made sure he had games on his phone that would work even in airplane mode. He'd brought a sketchbook, too, the most current version of the little one his uncle had gifted him all those years ago. He'd also brought that first one, carefully stowed away deep in his carry on.

He didn't have much room to draw, though, squeezed into the middle seat, so he put on headphones and played on his phone instead.

After he landed, he investigated the bus schedule and found one that would get him somewhat close to where he needed to be. There was a cheap motel not too far from his destination, he discovered, so he booked a room using the last dregs of power from his phone as he sat and swayed in his seat. It was marginally less uncomfortable than the airplane had been, at least.

The motel proved to be as disappointing as he'd feared. Wary of bedbugs, he set his suitcase on the lone chair rather than the bed, plugged in his phone, slung his backpack over his shoulder, and set out to find the house where Will had once lived and might have died.

~

Leo climbed up the familiar stairs, dragging his wheeled suitcase behind him with a series of hollow thumps. He set it down at the end of the bed and kicked off his shoes, settling crosslegged on the colorful quilt and looking around at the room. He glanced at the door, which had swung shut behind him, and said, "Will?"

For several long moments there was nothing, and Leo let out the breath he'd been holding. Will was kind of a weird ghost. Leo knew he was real, but he didn't know much about him. Leo wondered how long he'd been around, and what was keeping him in the world. He'd looked up stories about ghosts, but none of them had sounded anything like Will. In most stories ghosts were angry or vengeful or sad, but other than being a ghost, Will just seemed...normal. Like a normal guy Leo might meet anywhere.

A shimmer caught his attention, and he sat bolt upright. "Will!"

"Shh," Will's voice came, faint as wind rustling through the trees. "Don't worry. I told you, my grandma's half-deaf as it is. She's not going to notice me talking to someone, and if she does, I'll just tell her I was on the phone." He smiled with the air of one who had all the bases covered.

"Your parents are still downstairs," Will said, his voice still quiet.

Leo flopped back on the bed. "What are they *doing*? Doesn't their flight leave in just a couple of hours?"

The flickering presence winked out for a moment, then reappeared. "They're eating some of your grandma's pineapple upside down cake, it looks like."

"Oh, well, I can't blame them in that case." He felt his face twist into a frown. "Wait, there's *pineapple upside down cake*? I want some!" Jumping to his feet, he headed to the door, then stopped, his hand on the handle. "I won't be long, okay? I'll bring some —" It was on the tip of his tongue to offer to bring some for Will, but he caught himself just

71

in time. "I'll bring it back with me."

A soft glow suffused Will's presence for a split second, one that Leo kind of thought meant that Will was laughing even though it wasn't out loud. "I'll be here."

~

Leo hadn't thought too much about what he was going to say if someone opened the door. Somehow he'd imagined it would be an older person, maybe someone like his grandma, or perhaps his uncle.

He knocked on the door with firm confidence, his heart beating hard. He was used to flying by the seat of his pants and figured he could fake it no matter what response he got.

Unless, of course, there was no response. He frowned at the door and fidgeted, shifting his weight from one foot to the other. Glancing around, he saw that there was a doorbell. Should he ring it? Should he wait longer? He didn't want to be annoying. But maybe the inhabitants hadn't heard his knock? If they were hard of hearing like his grandma, they might need an extra-loud doorbell, or even the kind that flashed a light. He hesitated a little longer, then pressed the doorbell with his thumb. A distant two-tone electronic chime sounded, muffled by the wall and door, but distinctive enough to be a recognizable 'ding-dong'. There was a peephole, and Leo gazed at it nervously, hoping he didn't look like a creep.

...Still nothing. Should he come back later? Just as he was about to turn and go, the door swung open. He looked into the face of the house's inhabitant, slightly blurred by the screen door between them.

The first thing Leo noticed was that he wasn't old. He could have been anywhere from his late twenty to early thirties, but probably not more than that. He was thin and a little nerdy looking, with short black hair and dark eyes that were wide behind his wireframe glasses. His skin looked pallid against the dim interior behind him. After too-long moment where they stared at each other, he said, "Can I help you?"

"Uh, yes, sorry," Leo laughed. "I'm sorry to disturb you. I'm doing research for an article on these houses and the people who've lived in them over the years," he said quickly, picking the most straightforward of the approaches he'd been considering. "I wonder if I might ask you a few questions."

There was a wariness to the man as he studied Leo's face. Leo held his breath. He half-expected that he'd get the door slammed in his face. Instead, the screen door swung open in clear invitation.

"Very well. Please come in."

Leo let out his breath in a surprised whoosh. He was actually being invited in? This was even better than he'd hoped. "Thanks! I'll try not to take too much of your time."

"It's no trouble."

The house was small, but cozy. The front room seemed like it was a living room, but there was a kitchenette area off to the left side, a half-sized refrigerator and dishwasher taking up most of the space. Directly along the back wall was an ugly orange couch, more of a loveseat size than full-length. A crochet throw in rainbow colors was draped along the back. To the right were a couple of closed doors, and another door led off from the kitchen side as well, probably into the garage, Leo guessed. The space was dim compared to the brightness outside and had a slightly dusty, musty, bookish quality that reminded Leo of his grandmother's house.

Gesturing at the couch, the man said, "Please, have a seat." He twisted his hands together for a moment, then added with a strained air, "Can—can I get you some tea? Coffee?"

"Just a glass of water, if you don't mind." Leo had walked all the way there from the bus stop in the hot sun. He sank down onto the loveseat, feeling the cushions sag under his weight.

Nodding, the man went to the kitchenette and took out a glass, which he filled with water at the tap, then added two smaller-than-normal ice cubes from a miniature tray in the freezer. He also took out a saucer and set something on it before bringing it all to Leo, then awkwardly remained standing across from him. Leo juggled the plate of what turned out to be two store-bought almond cookies and the glass of water, setting the plate in his lap and taking a long drink from the glass. There was no coffee table or dining table or chairs. Leo guessed the man must eat his meals sitting on the couch, or maybe in his room. To be fair, so did Leo. Here there was no TV, though, just what looked like an ancient radio and record player in the corner.

"Do you want to sit down, too?" Leo asked, gesturing at the spot next to him. The loveseat was a little tight for complete strangers, but there was literally nowhere else to sit in the small room.

The couch sank even more as the man settled next to him. "What are your questions?" he said stiffly, his hands on his knees.

"Um, my name's Leo," he started. "Nice to meet you. Thank you for talking with me."

The man nodded. "Elijah," he said, and Leo couldn't help the self-deprecating smile that tugged at his lips as he bit back the urge to comment, *You don't look like an 'Elijah'*. After all, he didn't look much like a 'Leo', either.

"I'm looking for information about the people who lived," *and died* "in this house," he said. "How long have you lived here?"

"All my life," Elijah said. "My parents bought it years ago and they allowed me to stay in it when they moved away." He shrugged. "I couldn't possibly afford it otherwise."

"Oh, is it expensive?" Leo said, then grimaced at his misstep. If he was researching the houses as he was pretending to, surely he would have known that.

Fortunately, Elijah didn't seem to notice. He huffed out a little laugh. "This close to the ocean? Extremely expensive. This house is worth almost a hundred times what my parents paid for it decades ago."

Whistling, Leo looked around at the tiny place with a little more respect. "A hundred times?" He had no idea how much they'd paid originally, but if it was, say, fifty thousand back then, it would be valued at almost five million now. Even if they'd only paid ten thousand, it would be worth nearly a million dollars today, based on what Elijah had said. Leo resolved to do some research into local housing costs the next time he had access to free wifi. "Why didn't they sell it?"

Elijah cocked his head slightly, an endearing gesture. "I suppose they valued having a house near the ocean more than the money."

"And you?" Leo couldn't help asking, "If it was up to you, would you sell it?"

Blinking, Elijah said, "I don't know. I grew up here. I don't know where I would go if I sold it. I can't imagine living anywhere else."

"Still, it must be a tempting thought," Leo said wistfully. "Sounds like it would be enough money to live the rest of your life, maybe, if you're careful with it. You wouldn't have to work."

"I don't mind working," Elijah said.

"No? What do you do?"

"I'm a writer."

"Oh? Fiction or non-fiction?"

"Fiction. Fantasy novels, mostly." He rose from the couch, disappearing into one of the doors on the right, and returned a minute later to hand Leo a couple of paperbacks.

The covers were colorful and exciting, though Leo privately thought he could do better, his fingers itching for his sketchbook. He wouldn't have made the wizard's face quite so long, and the knight — king? — could have been more handsome. He didn't recognize any of the titles. "These look great."

"I can loan you one if you're interested," Elijah said.

"Really? I'd love that," Leo said, and meant it. Not only would he get free reading material, he would have a chance to further grill Elijah when he brought it back to return it. Speaking of which..."So, you said you've lived here all your life? When did your parents buy the house, do you know?"

Elijah pursed his lips, apparently mulling over the question. "I don't know the exact year, but I can find out."

"That would be great." Leo took a breath and reminded himself of why he was here. That was the problem with lying; it was easy to fall into the role and forget the goal. "I'm interested in everyone who's lived here, births, deaths, that kind of thing." Maybe Elijah had a brother who'd...passed away while his family had been visiting the town where Leo's grandma lived? It would fit all the circumstances, explaining why Will couldn't remember living there and why he'd always seemed close to Leo in age. Leo frowned to himself. Did ghosts age? They probably didn't *grow*, but they must be able to learn things and become more mature, at least based on his interactions with Will.

"I think my parents were the first owners of the house," Elijah said, "and as far as I know, no one's ever died here."

Leo nodded slowly. He couldn't just outright ask Elijah if he'd had a brother who'd died. That would be creepy *and* rude. But a desire to throw caution to the wind surged up like the tide. Taking a breath, he said, "Does the name 'Will' mean anything to you?"

No reaction. Elijah held himself as stiffly as before. "No," he said. "I'm sorry. It doesn't."

Frowning, Leo pressed, "Not at all? You don't have…that is, there aren't, or weren't, any family members by that name?"

Elijah met his eyes and slowly shook his head. "Not that I know of." His jaw was tight, his tone turning cold. "What is his significance to you?"

"Ah, um, it's not—" That was the other thing about lying. It trapped you into a single course. "Just—just someone I—that is, someone my family used to know. I think he might have lived here at some point."

"No." There was no room for compromise in Elijah's tone. "No one by that name lives here, or ever lived here, as far as I know."

~

They spent a lot of time exploring the forest. Even though grandma didn't own the land, Leo was allowed to wander through it to his heart's content, provided he didn't climb any fences.

He never had to worry about getting lost, either, as long as Will was there. Will could always lead them back, no matter how far they went off the regular trails.

"How do you do it?" Leo asked one day as he followed Will's witchlight glow through the dusk. It didn't actually brighten their surroundings at all, but it was easy to see against the darkening background, at least. They'd stayed out later than usual, and Leo knew his grandma would be worried. "How do you know where to go? Do you fly up high to see?"

"No, I just—I can just tell," Will admitted. "I can feel which way your grandma is, so I take you back to *her*, not the house."

"Huh." Leo picked his way across the uneven ground, hurrying as much as he dared. If he twisted his ankle it would take him even longer to get back, and then his grandma might forbid him from going into the forest alone. She'd been encouraging him to make friends with other kids his age in town. The few Leo had met had been all right, but he didn't know how to tell her that he liked Will better than any of them. Still, it *had* been fun to play video games again. One of the kids was rich, with his own TV and three different systems to play on, not to mention a ton of games. It was too bad Will couldn't come along. "What do you do when I'm not here?" Leo asked.

"In the summer, I explore other places. Watch the people and see what they do," Will said.

"Man, you really *would* be a good spy. You can get into all kinds of secret places and no one would ever know."

"No one except you," Will said, and Leo grinned.

"Yeah, we make a good team." His smile faded as he considered Will's words. "Do you have other friends in other places?" The thought made him feel strange.

"No," Will said. "You're still the only one who can see and hear me."

"Oh." That made Leo feel even weirder. He...kind of liked being the only one who could see or hear Will. But at the same time, it was kind of a responsibility. "You mean, I'm, like, your only friend?"

Will's shimmer drifted ahead a little, then paused, waiting for him. It was getting harder and harder to see the path ahead. "Yes," he said softly.

"Oh," Leo said again. "It's not fair," he added, frowning into the darkness.

"What's not?"

"I can have other friends, but you can't. Being a ghost kind of sucks."

"I don't mind. I'm glad that you and I can be friends."

"Thanks." Leo almost stumbled over a hidden root and flailed, catching himself just in time. "I guess there are good parts, though," he said as he righted himself. "You get to travel. You can go wherever you want! Right?"

"Yes," Will said.

"Have you ever been to Egypt?"

"Not yet. It's harder to find my way across long distances. Why Egypt?"

"We're learning about the Great Pyramid of Giza. Someday I'm gonna go there and see it for real." A thought struck him, and Leo grinned. "You can come with me! You won't even need a plane ticket!" He hesitated, "If you can find your way, that is."

"If you go, I'll try to go with you," Will said.

"It's a deal." The forest was thinning at last. Leo could see his grandma, standing at the edge with one hand gripping a flashlight and the other on her hip. "Grandma!" he said, and broke into a run. "I'm sorry I'm late!"

~

After meeting Elijah, Leo took his backpack with his trusty, battered laptop and charger and walked to the nearest coffee shop with free wifi.

It was a nice place, with outdoor tables that faced the street, just a few blocks down from the entrance to the beach. Leo ordered a small coffee, resolutely not looking at the pastries that would have cost his entire daily food budget, and settled in at a table along the periphery of the patio.

It didn't take him long to find all the public records available for Elijah's house. It had been built decades ago, and it looked like Elijah's family had been the only owners. Leo frowned at the screen. Why had Will given him that address?

Guilt surged through him. Had he ever even asked Will for his *last name?* They'd been 'Leo' and 'Will' from the start. To be fair, Will hadn't ever seemed like he *wanted* to talk about himself, steering the conversation to other things or telling Leo he didn't remember whenever Leo asked him anything personal.

But if he'd only pushed a little harder, maybe he would have more than an address and a first name to go off of. Sighing, Leo closed the laptop and dropped his empty mug off at the counter before heading down the street.

He felt unmoored. Some part of him had always intended to go back and see Will again. He'd thought Will would just—just be there. Waiting for him. When Leo had shown up each summer, Will had shimmered into existence as soon as Leo shut his door and quietly called his name.

Will had been such a good friend to him, and Leo had hardly tried to find out about him at all.

Walking faster, Leo made his way past the buildings and houses until suddenly, he had an unobstructed view of the ocean.

The sun was setting into it, turning the sky a blend of pinks and oranges and igniting the water into a blazing gold. Leo wandered off the sidewalk and up to the fence, peering down. A steep hillside covered in dark purple and bright yellow flowers led down to a sandy beach, people gathered in groups of twos and threes and mores along the golden strip between the hillside and the water. Couples walked arm in arm along the edge of the water, their feet bare. Children worked on sandcastles, jumping up as the tide washed over them.

He obviously wasn't supposed to try to clamber down the steep hillside, so Leo followed the fence instead until he came to a zig-zagging cement staircase that led down to the sand. He started down, making his way past tired families carrying or coaxing exhausted children, a surfer in a black wetsuit who carried a longboard under his arm, and a gaggle of teenagers—what was the plural noun for teenagers? an 'annoyance'?—an annoyance of teenagers who were giggling and shouting at each other.

The idea of heading back to his motel held little appeal, and the light looked like it would last a bit longer. Leo hunted in his backpack for his phone, but ended up pulling out one of the paperbacks Elijah had loaned him instead. Shrugging, Leo settled onto the sand and started to read.

~

The good thing about Will was that Leo could tell him anything. Leo had told him a lot of things over the years, even about things he'd been ashamed of. It was just easier to talk to someone who didn't have a face, and who didn't try to interrupt or tell you what you should do about your problem.

His grandma had packed him a picnic. After a few years of trying to get him to be more social with the other kids in town, she'd finally accepted that Leo's preferred activity was wandering through the forest 'alone'.

It didn't take long to find one of their favorite spots, a stream with a bend in it that curved around a huge boulder. The boulder had been weathered and smoothed by time, graffitied at least once, but the paint had since mostly faded and washed away. "Stupid," Leo said running his fingers over the paint that remained. "If you want it to stay, you gotta use primer."

"For graffiti?" There was a laugh in Will's voice, and Leo found himself chuckling in response.

"Sure, why not? Who would suspect you weren't supposed to be doing it if you came out with a can of primer and a brush? Heck, you could use a can of paint and a brush, too. I bet no one would even stop you."

"You're not thinking of doing it, are you?" Now Will sounded caught between amusement and alarm.

Snorting, Leo shook his head. "Or course not." He pulled himself up onto the top of the rock and settled into a crosslegged position to pull out his lunch. A roast beef sandwich, some carrots from her little garden, and three homemade chocolate chip cookies. His grandma really was the best.

"You said you wanted to tell me something?"

The roast beef suddenly felt hard to swallow. Leo's stomach twisted a little. "Yeah," he said, putting down the sandwich. He took a breath and forced himself to say it out loud. "I just, um. I thought you should know that I'm. That I." He rubbed a hand along the back of his neck.

"What is it?" Will said, barely audible over the rushing of the creak.

"I'm gay," Leo said at last. "I like guys."

Will was silent, his shimmer seeming to slow for a second. Finally he said, sounding cautious, "Okay."

"Are you—do you—you don't care, right?" Leo said.

"No." Will's shimmer made a jerking motion that Leo had come to associate with nervousness. "I am—that is—I think, I think I might have been, too."

"*Really?*" Will was? *Will* had been? "You were? You're not just saying that to make me feel better or something stupid like that, right?"

"Of course not!" Will sounded offended. "I wouldn't lie about something like that!"

"No, I guess not. It's just, I didn't expect it. I thought—how old were you when you died, anyway? How long had you known?"

"You know I don't remember," Will said impatiently, then added, his voice calmer, "And I don't know how I knew. I just...figured it out, I guess."

"Huh." Leo picked up his sandwich again, chewing and swallowing thoughtfully. "You figured it out as a *ghost*?" A gay ghost, that was just, it was *weird*. He hastily squashed the thought before he could voice it and hurt Will's feelings. Another thought struck him, and he blinked.

Did Will like *him*? Will said he'd 'figured it out', maybe it had been because they'd spent so much time together?

The thought swirled around in Leo's brain as he finished his lunch. Will didn't speak.

Did it matter? Will was a ghost. It wasn't like they could be together anyway.

When he was done, Leo packed up the trash into his backpack, slung it over his shoulders, and clambered his way down the boulder.

"Let's head back," he said.

"Sure," Will said, his voice even and quiet.

~

The novel was great.

Leo was drawn in immediately, rooting for the main characters and disgusted by the evil people they were fighting. He made it through several chapters before it grew too dark to read anymore and the breeze off the ocean picked up, making him shiver. At least the staircase leading up from the beach was well-lit, though the lights were those greenish-yellow ones that made everything look strange and washed out. Even so, he was tempted to perch himself on one of the landings and keep reading, but he had a feeling that he might get in trouble for loitering if he did that. With a sigh, he tucked the book away.

He had an idea where it was going anyway. He could have sworn he hadn't read it before, but somehow, it felt familiar, like he knew the story even if he'd never read it. Maybe it *had* been one of the titles he'd checked out of some library years ago? Stopping and fishing it out of his backpack again, he checked the publication date—just four years ago. No, he definitely would have remembered it. Maybe the author had drawn on some myth Leo had studied at some point.

He was in the middle of putting the book away again when it occurred to him that he knew the author. He could *ask* him.

Grinning, he hurried back to his hotel, picking up some snacks from a gas station convenience store on the way.

~

"I can't," Leo groaned.

"You gotta," Will said, sounding panicked. "Leo, you gotta try. You can use a stick to lean on, come on."

Groaning, Leo levered himself up once more. He didn't dare try to put any weight on his leg again. Instead he leaned against a tree, balancing on his right leg. "I think it's broken."

Will made a worried sound. "Try your cell phone again."

Leo dug in his pocket and pulled out his phone, holding it out so Will could see the shattered screen. "It's dead. I tried turning it back on twice already." As loath as Leo was to admit it, Will had been right. He shouldn't have tried climbing down that steep hillside. Still, what kind of bad luck was it that he'd not only tripped on a root and tumbled down to the bottom, but managed to break both his leg *and* his cell phone in the process?

"All right." Will sounded on the verge of panicking. Weirdly, Leo wasn't scared at all. It *hurt*, but he knew his grandma would send people to look for him if he didn't show up when it started to get dark. They'd find him eventually.

He wondered if there were any wild animals that came out at night.

Okay, maybe he was a little scared.

"Will?" he said.

"I'm here." Will's voice was distracted. "I'm trying to think what to do, hang on."

His shimmer faded to nothing for a few minutes, which wasn't unusual when he was 'thinking'. Sometimes he would disappear without warning, other times he'd say he had to leave. Will had teased him about it more than once—what could Will have to do that was so important? He was a *ghost*—but Will never told him why or where he went.

Leo closed his eyes and forced his breathing steady. He tried to take a step with the branch he'd picked up as a makeshift crutch, but it was no use. He could hop a little while, but there was no way he could make it back up that hillside. And in the other direction was a river, not exceptionally deep or fast-flowing, but enough to make Leo nervous even when he *didn't* have a broken leg. No way was he going to try to cross it like this.

A familiar prickly sensation brushed against the back of his hand, pins and needles and the static of a freshly-laundered blanket. "Leo?"

"I don't think I can make it," he said, fighting the way his throat tried to close. "I'm going to have to wait until someone finds me." He swallowed hard. "Stay with me?"

"Of course. For as long as I can. Don't worry, your grandma will definitely send someone."

Nodding, Leo settled carefully onto the ground, his back against the tree. "Thanks."

"I had a new idea for a story the other day, did I tell you?"

"No." Leo leaned his head back and closed his eyes. They didn't play make believe games anymore, but Will still always came up with the best ideas. Someday they were going to make something together, maybe a movie or a comic book or something.

"Okay, it's in a fantasy world," Will started. "There's this prince…"

~

Leo stayed up late finishing the book, crashing after midnight and sleeping late into the morning. The cheap place he was staying didn't even have air conditioning. He woke up sweating and desperate for a shower.

Once he was as clean as he could get under the lukewarm trickle from the crappy showerhead, he checked the forecast. The weather had been mild yesterday, but it looked like they were headed for a hot spell. Leo made a face and debated going back to the beach again to read the other novel Elijah had loaned him, but ultimately decided he would head back to Elijah's house and return the first novel instead. Talking with the writer had left him feeling…odd. Elijah had been so tense the entire time Leo had been there. Leo wondered why Elijah had even invited him in, especially given that Leo's request for information hadn't required anything of the sort. While he'd appreciated the hospitality (and the water and cookies) it had been unexpected, and hadn't seemed to come to Elijah naturally. He'd been awkward, even uncomfortable.

And yet, there'd been something positive about the interaction. Not just getting to borrow one of his books, but before that. Some people just gave one a good feeling—'good vibes', Leo's mom called it. Despite his shyness and obvious discomfort, there was something about Elijah, something that made Leo want to be near him, to talk with him, and to put him at ease if he could.

Then there was the issue of Will. Had he been lying about his address? Or perhaps he'd mis-remembered? Maybe Leo had written it down wrong, perhaps it was 557 instead of 577 or something ridiculous like that. Leo bit at a hangnail on his thumb, the little sting of pain echoing his frustration. Why, *why* hadn't he pushed Will for a little more? Why hadn't he tried to come and see him during his travels? Leo'd been so excited to go overseas, he'd barely even thought about going back to his grandma's. Had hardly thought about how he'd left Will alone, too caught up in the whirl of his own life.

Shaking his head, he let his hand fall to his side, then crouched and slung his backpack over his shoulder. First, he would return the novel. Then he would do some more research. Maybe there was a different Ocean View Drive. It was probably a common street name this close to the coast.

The bus ride wasn't long, but between sleeping in and taking his time in the shower, the wait for the bus and the walk from the bus stop, by the time he'd made his way from the bus stop to Elijah's door it was almost three o'clock. Leo regretted not bringing a hat or some sunscreen.

This time he remembered to ring the doorbell. It didn't take as long for the door to swing inward, revealing Elijah in a t-shirt and what looked like lightweight slacks. "You're back?" he said, his expression startled. For a second, a small smile touched his lips before he stiffened again. "Come in, let me get you some water."

Leo smiled back and made his way to the couch. The small house didn't seem to have air conditioning, but the dim interior of the living room was considerably cooler than outside. There was only one window, a large, westward facing one at the front of the house, but it was covered by a cream-colored curtain that only let a thinned and filtered light into the room. Elijah pressed a cold glass into Leo's hand and handed him another saucer with two almond cookies in an echo of yesterday's visit. "Thanks," Leo said, taking a gulp of water and closing his eyes for a moment as the cool liquid washed down his throat.

"What brings you back so soon?" Elijah said, perching next to him on the loveseat. "Did you learn more about the house's history?"

Guilt stabbed through Leo. He felt his smile falter and turn rueful. "Ah, uh, no. I mean, I did do a little research, but I mainly came back to return one of the novels you loaned me."

"Oh." Elijah blinked as Leo fished the book out of his backpack. He'd done his best to keep it in good condition, treating it far more carefully than his usual quarter-a-paperback finds from used bookstores. Elijah accepted it with a nod. "You finished it already? Or did you not like it?"

"I loved it!" Leo said.

Elijah's fingers tightened on the book, his eyes widening a little. "You did?"

"Yeah. It really," Leo frowned, searching for words, "it resonated with me. I liked the relationship between the main characters, like how you made the prince more of a hermit and the wizard outgoing and friendly, switched things up from how people usually do it."

Elijah smiled down at the cover, his cheeks rounding and the corners of his eyes wrinkling behind his glasses. It made him look boyish, sweeter. Leo blinked. How old was Elijah, anyway? Leo had guessed that he was in his late twenties, perhaps even his thirties, but looking at him again, especially his smooth hands and unlined face, he re-evaluated his estimate to closer to the first than the second.

Definitely under twenty-five.

"I-I'm glad you liked it," Elijah said. "Would you like to borrow another?"

"I still have the second one you loaned me yesterday," Leo said. "But when I finish that one, I would absolutely like to borrow more. How many have you written?"

"Five," Elijah said. "I'm almost done with my sixth."

"Wow." Leo absently picked up one of the cookies and bit into it. "How old are you, anyway, if you don't mind my asking?"

"I'm twenty-three," Elijah said, and Leo almost dropped the cookie.

"You have five, almost six published novels, and you're only twenty-three? Jeez, what the hell am I doing with my life?" He shook his head and shoved the rest of the cookie in his mouth.

"I didn't go to college," Elijah said, sounding apologetic. "And I don't—that is—I don't do much else other than write. Your life is probably much more interesting."

Leo snorted and polished off the glass of water. "Interesting, maybe, but aimless." He let his head tilt up against the back of the couch, staring at the ceiling. "I have one more year of college, but I have no idea what I want to do with my life."

Elijah didn't say anything for a long moment. Finally he put his hands on his knees and squeezed them, then took a breath. "Well," he said at last, "what do you like doing?"

"Traveling," Leo said promptly. "I've spent five of the past six summers traveling, staying in hostels, taking odd jobs, and just going from place to place. Seeing everything there is to see." Sour frustration rose in him. "But you can't make a living doing that."

A furrow appeared between Elijah's brows. "You could be a travel writer."

"Hah, not a bad idea," Leo said. "Except that I'm not good with words and I'm not good with deadlines." He gave a half-shrug. "I'm pretty good at drawing, but that's *really* hard to make a living at."

"But doesn't your—" Elijah started, then stopped short and dropped his eyes. "That is—maybe you could make sketches of each place you go and put them together in a book or something?"

"Who would buy something like that?" Leo said bitterly, and

shook his head. "I guess I could start something online, posting drawings of places I've been." His gaze drifted to his backpack, where his sketchbook was tucked into the front pocket. "But that would be something I'd have to update regularly. I think it would get stressful really fast."

"I see." Elijah gave a determined nod. "I'll think on it."

"It's not up to you to figure out a career for me," Leo said with a laugh. He rolled his shoulders and his head, cracking his neck. "I'm majoring in engineering. It's not too bad. I'll probably just get a job like everyone else in the world and spend a couple of weeks of vacation traveling every year."

"That doesn't sound like it would make you happy," Elijah said quietly.

Shrugging, Leo said, "Is anyone really happy? Are you?"

Elijah pursed his lips and Leo found his gaze narrowing in on them. "I suppose I would say that I'm content," Elijah said, breaking the spell. Leo blinked and gave himself a little shake. "But I'm not sure happiness is possible for someone like me. I think you could have a chance at it, though."

"What do you mean, 'someone like you'?" Leo let his eyes sweep over the other man. He seemed to be in good health, thin but not excessively so, his skin pale but not sickly, his dark eyes clear and his hair neatly-combed but not limp. Suddenly acutely aware of their close proximity on the loveseat, Leo pulled his elbows in and shifted slightly.

"I'm not..." Elijah's tongue flicked over his lips. "That is, I don't usually –" he stopped abruptly, the furrow in his forehead returning, deeper than before. "I'd rather not discuss it," he said, some of his earlier stiffness returning.

"Ah, okay," Leo said hastily. "I'm sorry, I didn't mean to pry. It's none of my business."

"It's fine," Elijah said. He made a sharp gesture with his hand, as though sweeping aside all that had been said before. "But it's different for you. You have options. You could – you can do more. You can do what you want. Why shouldn't you?"

Leo's chest felt tight. "To tell you the truth," he said, and stopped, swallowing. Elijah didn't speak, just waited for him to go on. "To tell you the truth," Leo repeated, "My grandma died recently."

"Oh," Elijah said. His eyes went wide, then he looked away uncomfortably. "I didn't know. I'm sorry."

"It's — she lived a good life," Leo said. "A long, good life. I, she, I used to spend summers at her house. And she left a lot of things to my mom and my uncle, but she — she left the house to me." He felt Elijah's full attention on him, laser-focused in its intensity. "I'm not sure what to do," he finished, embarrassed by how shaky his voice came out.

After a moment or two, Elijah said, "What to do?"

"Yeah." Leo squeezed his eyes shut. "I love that old place. Every summer for years — " He stopped, shaking his head. "I know what I should do. I should live there, get a job in the city, commute in and out every day. Not too many people my age own a house. I'm lucky. Or else I should sell it and pay off the rest of my student loans, then whatever's left will be a nest egg, I guess to buy another house someday," he said, finishing on a wry note. He rolled the empty glass back and forth between his palms.

"And what do you want to do?"

"I want — I do want to pay off my loans. I know grandma was hoping I would, she said so in the letter she left for me. But if there's anything left over," he couldn't help the shudder that shook through him, the longing. "I want to travel more. At least for a few more years. Just — just go wherever I can, anywhere I can get a cheap flight or find a place to stay. I've done it every summer for the past several years, and I've never been happier. Except when — " *Except when I was with Will*, he thought, the memories warm and golden in his mind's eye. He swallowed back the words.

"Except — ?"

Shaking his head, Leo said, "It doesn't matter. Anyway, it's a stupid dream. Wasting everything that I put into college, everything my parents tried to do for me. How selfish can I get? And that house — how can I think of selling it? Even if I can travel, I'm going to need a place to come home to." He gave a miserable laugh. "I can't just throw everything away."

"Your parents," Elijah said slowly, "don't they want you to be happy?"

"Of course they do!" Leo said, his voice louder than he'd meant it to be. Hot anger pressed against his chest. Elijah didn't react, just watched him with dark eyes, his expression unreadable. "Of course they do," Leo repeated, softening his tone. "I guess we just have different ideas about what that means."

Lifting a hand, Elijah gripped his shoulder. "Talk to them," he said, the gentleness of his words contrasting with the hard weight on his shoulder. Leo leaned into the touch; it was grounding, anchoring. "Just talk to them. You've—you've been able to talk to them before, haven't you?"

"Yeah," Leo said. "They're actually pretty great." He let his head droop, hanging heavy on his neck. "I'm being an idiot, aren't I? Most people in college would kill to have my dilemma. Poor me, should I pay off my loans or keep a place to live, my life is so awful!" he said, infusing his words with melodrama. Snorting, he dropped the tone and said, "Talk about a First World problem."

A huff of laughter made him look up. Elijah was smiling again, his eyes gleaming behind their thin layer of glass, his cheeks lightly flushed. "You're allowed to want something different from what everyone else thinks you should want," he said. "It doesn't make you selfish."

"Doesn't it?" Leo said. Elijah just shook his head. "But—" Leo stopped, feeling his forehead crease into a frown. "Wanting something different from what everyone else thinks I should..."

Oh. It wasn't like he was going to get married and have two and a half kids someday. For most of his life, he'd wanted something other than the 'norm'.

"I guess I—I really am an idiot."

"You're *not*," Elijah said, sounding a little exasperated. "You're fine. Don't call yourself that." He let go of Leo's shoulder, placing his hand on his own knee once more.

"Anyway," Leo said awkwardly, "I, uh, I really just came to return the novel I borrowed, not to get life advice. I hope I didn't disturb you. Were you writing?"

"No, I usually write in the morning and sometimes after lunch," Elijah said. "Your timing was actually very good."

"Good. That's good. Uh, if it's all right," Leo fished around for his cell phone in his backpack, "can I get your number? That way I can text you before I come over to return the other book and you can tell me if it's a bad time."

"Yes," Elijah said. "Just a moment." He rose from the loveseat and disappeared into one of the doors as Leo pulled up the phone dialer.

"What's your number?" Leo said as Elijah returned with a shiny, new-looking phone in his hand.

There was a moment of hesitation. "I don't remember it," Elijah admitted.

Leo laughed, glad of the break in tension. "New phone? I've been there. Here, you can call me, then I'll have your number and you'll have mine."

Nodding, Elijah began to tap at his phone with the clumsiness of someone who wasn't at all familiar with it, his eyes darting desperately around the screen.

"Want me to do it? I've used a lot of different cell phones while traveling," Leo offered, and Elijah sighed in obvious relief before handing over the device.

It didn't take long to program both numbers in, noting that Elijah hadn't transferred over any of his old contacts, leaving his list blank except for one entry called "Mom" and one called "Publisher". Leo handed Elijah back his phone, saying, "There, now I can let you know before I'm coming. Y'know, you can get them to transfer your old contact list at the cell place." He glanced down at his own phone and felt his back go stiff. "Is that the time? Crap, I've gotta go if I'm gonna catch the next bus. The one after isn't for another hour and a half." He started shoving his phone back in his backpack.

"Where are you staying?" Elijah asked as Leo was slinging his backpack over his shoulder. When Leo named the motel, Elijah made a face. "Not *there*? That place is awful!"

"I've stayed in worse," Leo said.

"That doesn't make me feel better! The police have busted that place at least twice for illegal drug deals and, and — and other things!"

"That explains why it's so cheap," Leo said with a shrug. "Don't worry, I'm careful. Always lock my door, and I know the tricks for avoiding bed bugs."

"Bed *bugs!*" Elijah said. His expression of horror was priceless.

"I've actually only encountered them once," Leo said, grinning.

"Leo! You can't stay there!"

"Hey, I'm fine, truly," Leo said soothingly. "Really. I'm not going to get knifed or eaten alive or something. At worst I'll get some fleabites and sweat a lot." He turned to leave, but Elijah darted forward and caught hold of his sleeve.

"Stay here," he said.

Leo stopped. "What?"

"Stay here," Elijah said. "I have an extra room, with a bed and everything. My parents' room, it's fine, a little dusty maybe, but there are *definitely* no bed bugs or — "

"Elijah, you barely know me," Leo said, chuckling. "You can't just invite me to stay in your house."

"I can and I am," Elijah said, raising his chin. "Stay here. I won't charge you anything. How long will you be in town for?"

~

"I told them."

Will flickered next to him. Leo had spent the past week mostly stuck in bed, hobbling around his grandma's house on crutches and struggling up and down the stairs. He was getting better at it, at least.

Thank goodness Will was here. Leo would have been going stir-crazy if he'd had to spend the time alone. His grandma was nice, but there were only so many games of parcheesi and backgammon one could play. She'd tried to teach him bridge, and he'd tried to teach her poker, but neither of them were particularly adept teachers, especially when they could only half-remember the rules themselves.

With Will, though, things were always easy. Usually Leo liked to read, but the painkillers made the words slide away from him and he found his mind wandering when he tried. When Will offered to read to him, it was different. Leo found he could just curl up, letting Will's voice carry him, turning the page whenever Will's tingling, electric touch brushed over the back of his hand.

Honestly, Leo had been lucky. It turned out someone had called an ambulance; probably someone who lived inside one of those fenced-in areas in the woods, he'd figured. Apparently they'd some-how seen Leo fall and had called for help, so the paramedics had ended up coming for him much sooner than he'd expected them to, long before dark. They'd helped him contact his grandma, too. It had been such a relief when they'd shown up, it had taken everything he'd had not to burst into tears.

Now he was stuck with a cast on his leg for the last few weeks of the summer, which sucked, but things could have been a lot worse. The paramedics had even praised him, telling him that waiting for help had been the right thing to do, rather than risking aggravating his injury. Leo just wished he knew who had called for help so he could send them a thank-you note.

Being unable to go outside had left him with a lot of time on his hands, time he'd mostly spent with Will, but there'd been some time to think, too.

He took another breath and let it out. "I came out to my parents." He'd told them on the phone last night, after Will had 'gone to bed'. (For a ghost, he seemed to weirdly dislike the dark. Every night around when the summer sun was going down, he would tell Leo that he had to leave.)

Now Will's shimmer intensified, the flickers getting faster. "What did they say?"

Leo gave a little laugh at the memory. "My mom scolded me for telling them over the phone because she couldn't hug me long distance. My dad thanked me and said he'd just won ten bucks. I guess they'd bet on when I would come out to them."

"They knew." Will's tone was more amused than surprised.

"Yeah. I asked why they never said anything, and my mom said that they hadn't wanted to push me. My dad said he didn't want to lose the bet."

Will's bright, clear laughter rang in Leo's ears, lifting his heart along with it.

~

Elijah was insistent and surprisingly intense. "I don't even use the room," he said, swinging the door open.

Leo had been both right and wrong: the door next to the kitchenette led to the garage, but the garage wasn't a garage anymore. It had been converted into an absolutely beautiful space. Though he remembered seeing an ordinary garage door from the outside, someone had walled it up from the inside, and cut a large window into the back wall opposite, letting in the late afternoon sunshine and looking out into a postage stamp-sized yard. "The light must be fantastic in the morning," Leo said, gazing at the east-facing window.

"It is," Elijah said. "You can draw or paint in here if you like."

The space was bright and open, much more so than the dim interior of the main room. What had originally been a one-car garage had been divided, with a small walled off section that looked like it was probably a bathroom on the far side of the room. On the left, next to where the garage door had been filled in, was a queen-sized bed. It was covered in a white duvet, two pillows arranged at the head with symmetrical perfection.

The rest of the walls were covered with white-painted bookshelves crammed with double-stacked books, mostly paperbacks. Beneath the window on the right was a large desk, perfect for sketching or drawing or placing a laptop on.

"Elijah," Leo breathed, "This is gorgeous." Turning, he caught a relieved smile on Elijah's lips. "But why," Leo said, "*why* aren't you renting this out to someone? If houses in this area are worth so much, a separate room like this, with its own bathroom, must rent for a ton."

The smile faded, and Elijah shrugged. "I wouldn't feel comfortable living with someone else," he said, quickly adding, "long-term, I mean. I'm happy to have you here, though. You can stay as long as you like."

Was it Leo's imagination, or was there a faint emphasis on the 'you' in that sentence?

Before he could say anything else, Elijah said, "I need to order groceries. Is there anything you'd like me to add?"

"'Order' groceries? You're not getting them delivered, are you?"

Tilting his head to one side in that endearing way, Elijah said, "Is there a reason I shouldn't?"

"It's just so expensive," Leo fretted. "Between the delivery fee and the tip, not to mention that they jack up the price on some things compared to buying them in the store."

Shrugging, Elijah said, "I'm willing to pay for the convenience."

Leo made a face. "It's such a waste, though." An idea struck him. "Hey, I can go for you, if you want! As long as you don't want to buy more than I can carry, that is." Elijah was single and lived alone; he probably didn't buy that many groceries at a time.

"I usually place a large order and stock up so I don't have to think about it," Elijah said. Leo deflated. It would have been nice to be able to help out and save Elijah some cash. "I do have a car, though," Elijah said. "I could...drop you off at the store?"

"If it's not too much trouble. I'm trying to help, not make your life *more* complicated," Leo said sheepishly.

"It's fine. I don't mind driving, as long as I don't have to go inside the store." His gaze swept over Leo and around the room, landing on Leo's backpack. "Is that all of your luggage?"

"No, I left my suitcase back at the motel. I'm already going to have to pay for tonight anyway, since I missed the checkout window, so I'll take the bus over and grab it tomorrow."

"We can stop there on the way to the store," Elijah said. "No need to leave it there any longer than necessary."

It was clear that Elijah wouldn't take 'no' for an answer. "All right. Thank you again." He wasn't sure why Elijah was prepared to help him out, or so invested in his well-being. Hopefully Leo could find ways to repay his kindness.

Of course, his family would probably warn Leo that *he* was the one who needed to be careful. For all he knew, Elijah was a mass-murderer and would bury Leo in his backyard. Leo had done some wild things, but staying with a *complete* stranger, one that wasn't at least a friend-of-a-friend, was a new height of risk. He resolved to send an email to his family that night letting them know where he was staying. They were used to him dropping everything at a moment's notice to jump on a cheap airfare deal or flitting off to chase something that caught his attention. They probably wouldn't be *too* surprised that he'd ended up on the other side of the country after telling them he was going to grandma's house.

He wouldn't tell them that Elijah was a stranger, he decided. They would only nag him, and he couldn't give them a good reason for why he wasn't worried. There was just something about Elijah. Leo found himself relaxing in his presence, despite the tension he could sense in the set of Elijah's shoulders and jaw. It was weirdly comfortable being around him. Almost easy. It didn't make sense. But Leo couldn't make himself believe that Elijah was dangerous or a bad person. The idea felt laughable.

"When should we go?" Leo asked.

"Whenever you like," Elijah said. "Now, if you want."

"Sure, now is good. No time like the present, right?"

"Let me just write a list." He smiled a little. "I haven't been to the grocery store in years. I might have to get directions."

"Really? Years? Not even to pick up something you forgot?"

Giving a one-shouldered shrug, Elijah said, "I really don't like shopping."

"Why not? Did something awful happen to you in a grocery store?" Leo said lightly.

"No." Elijah replied as though it had been a serious question, but the quirk at the corner of his mouth betrayed his amusement. The quirk faded as he shrugged again and finished awkwardly, "I just don't like it."

"Well, I don't mind it," Leo declared. "As long as I'm staying here, I can save you some money by doing the shopping." He chuckled and rubbed the back of his neck. "As long as you can give me rides to the store, that is."

~

"Where do you go everyday?" Leo asked, gazing down at the carved wooden pieces his grandfather had fashioned. They were simple, with just enough detail to differentiate them.

"Pawn to e4," Will said, and Leo moved the white piece for him. "What do you mean, where do I go?"

"I used to think you left when the sun went down. But I've been watching, and it's always at eight o'clock at night. You always leave at eight. Except that one time, when you came back." Leo had been miserable, his broken leg aching. Will had left as usual, but later he'd returned and read to Leo until Leo had finally fallen asleep. "Where do you go?"

"I don't...I don't know," Will said.

95

The 'white' and 'black' pawns were really just two different shades of brown, one treated with a light stain that left the wood almost the original color, while the other had been dyed quite dark. Sliding his own 'black' pawn to e5, Leo said, "Maybe you have to go back to heaven? Or," he swallowed, "You don't have to go to hell, do you?"

"No! Nothing like that."

"How do you know? If you don't remember where you go, how do you know it's not hell?"

"I just do. It doesn't feel like it's somewhere bad or scary. Just— just somewhere I have to go."

"Maybe it's your grave," Leo whispered.

"Maybe," Will said, but he sounded dubious.

"I wish you could remember."

Will was quiet. "Knight to f3," he said at last, and Leo snorted and moved the piece. Chess had been a good idea. They'd had much more success with it than their early abortive attempts at board games, especially once they'd learned the shorthand for it. But then Will had somehow read a bunch of chess strategy books, which forced Leo to look up a bunch of strategy hints on the internet in self-defense. It made the early parts of their games less exciting, but Will always insisted that they play out every turn, even when Leo could tell which opening he was using from the first move. "Does it matter so much, where I go?" Will said. "You usually go to sleep anyway, right?"

"When I was younger, sure. But now I usually stay up until at least ten."

"No wonder you're always so out of it in the mornings," Will said, chuckling. When he laughed, it always made him shimmer faster. Leo felt his own lips turning up in response. He automatically moved his own knight to c6 and waited for Will's next move, knowing it would be 'bishop to b5'.

"Bishop to b5," Will said, and Leo rolled his eyes, moving the piece.

"I guess it doesn't matter," Leo said, trying to focus on the board. "As long as you're okay and not, like, hurting or something." He let his hand hover over his pieces, then pulled it back as an idea struck him. "What if you're living two different lives? Well, not living, but, like. Experiencing." He looked over at Will's glimmering presence.

"Actually, that would be a good idea for a story, wouldn't it?"

"One person living two lives?"

"Yeah, except, he doesn't *know* it."

"I like it," Will said. "Does he just not sleep, or?"

"Hm, magic or tech? Maybe tech?"

"A techno-thriller," Will said, his voice quickening with enthusiasm. "He's got implants that switch his mind from one set of memories to the other. But there's some sort of bleed-through, and he doesn't know which 'self' is the real one."

"Yeah!" Leo said. He grabbed for his sketchbook and started drawing a man with wires coming out of the back of his neck.

~

Elijah's grocery list was neat, precise, and specific, complete with brand names and sizes, as well as alternatives in case the store was sold out. A couple of times Leo was tempted to swap something out for a cheaper version—why were Fuji apples TWICE as expensive as Galas?—but in the end he figured that Elijah would prefer him to stick to the list as closely as possible.

He sent Elijah a text when he got in line to check out, fully expecting that he would be waiting at least five minutes in front of the store with the full cart. To his surprise, Elijah was already parked, sitting in his car with his head bent over a book. Leo frowned.

"Thanks," he said, after Elijah got out to help him load the groceries into the trunk. "But did you even leave? Or did you just stay in the car the whole time? I was trying to help you, not make things more difficult," he added as he handed over the receipt and the change from the cash Elijah had insisted he take.

"You did help me," Elijah said, glancing at the receipt. "You were right, it was considerably cheaper this way. I'd planned to spend the evening reading anyway, it didn't matter where."

"But—" Leo sighed and shook his head. "All right, if you say so."

Elijah started the car and Leo let his gaze rest out the window, watching as Elijah smoothly navigated the traffic during the short drive back to his house.

It didn't take long to put the food away. Leo had only purchased about a bag's worth for himself. Mindful of Elijah's tiny fridge, he'd mostly chosen inexpensive non-perishables. Elijah cleared a shelf for him in one of his neatly-organized cabinets, and Leo stuck everything in, pleased that it all fit.

After that, Leo took a proper shower in the private little bathroom built into the garage-turned-master bedroom, threw on his cleanest t-shirt and pair of shorts, and wandered back to the main room.

Elijah was sitting cross-legged on the love seat, book in one hand. He'd changed as well, into a t-shirt and sweatpants. He looked softer, like this, more approachable. Quiet music drifted through the room, some gentle orchestral piece, and Leo noted that the record player in the corner was spinning. Elijah looked up at him and smiled.

There was no reason the expression should make the breath catch in Leo's chest. Just because it was the most relaxed expression he'd ever seen on Elijah's face, just because Elijah seemed genuinely *happy*, was no reason for *Leo's* heart to speed up, for his face to heat, for his fingertips to start tingling.

Leo knew himself. He fell sudden and hard for people. He'd had a number of flings during his travels—brief, intense interludes that burned bright and died fast. But this—this didn't feel the same. It had always begun with a sharp hunger, with *desire* swamping him, careening out of control. It was always a wild ride until it invariably crashed and burned.

This wasn't that. This was something else. He wanted to cup his hands around the feeling, both to warm them and to shield it like a candle flame from the wind.

What the hell? He'd known Elijah for less than forty-eight hours! Lust would have been comprehensible, easy to deal with. Lust meant binary choices: say something or not, act on it or not. But Leo had no idea where the desire to go and *lay his head in Elijah's lap* was coming from, and therefore no idea how to react to it.

The warm smile faded into a look of inquiry, and Leo realized he'd been staring. "I'm, uh, gonna go read the other novel you loaned me," he said.

"Ah. I hope you like it," Elijah said. "It's a different genre from the other one."

"I'm sure I will." Stiffly, Leo went to the kitchen and got himself a glass of water, drank it while standing next to the sink, rinsed the glass and put it away. He could feel Elijah's eyes on him the entire time.

Back in his bedroom with the door safely closed, he sat on his borrowed bed and gave himself a shake.

He wasn't going to be staying here long. Whatever that had been, it didn't matter. He wouldn't let it matter. Reaching for his backpack, he dug out the second novel Elijah had loaned him and settled back to start reading it.

It was good, good enough to distract him even from his awkward and unexpected surge of emotion. Unlike the last book, this one was a techno thriller. It featured two spies, partners who worked together. One was a tech wiz, the other was the muscle. The story was told from the point of view of the tech half of the pair, the one who saw everything through cameras and heard everything through microphones. Leo was quickly drawn into the world, feeling the tech's despair when his partner was hurt and the tech couldn't get to him or help him, sharing his triumph when he found a way out and got his partner to safety.

It wasn't a genre Leo read that often. He was picky about stories set in the 'real world', less willing to accept fancy technological explanations than he was when the answer was simply 'magic'. But like the fantasy he'd read yesterday (had it only been yesterday?) it felt oddly familiar. He couldn't quite predict what would come next, and yet, and *yet*, little details hit him with a vivid sense of recognition. When the techie led his partner through the enemy's compound, no more than a voice in his ear, it was almost visceral. As though he'd been there, done that exact thing himself.

He stayed up too late reading again, but didn't quite finish the book.

~

"You're doing fine." Will's voice was encouraging.

Leo glared down at his feet. The river water washed around his calves, a constant but varying pressure. It was fairly clear here, but any deeper and he wouldn't be able to see the bottom.

"Want to try another step?" Will said. "You're still very shallow."

"All right." Gingerly, Leo lifted his foot and lowered it slowly, testing the bottom with his toes before putting his full weight on it. The sound of Will's laugh made heat rise in his face. "*What?*"

"Sorry. You just look like an old-time bathing beauty or something, dipping your toe in the water. Or a woman in a cartoon standing on a chair to get away from a mouse."

"Oh, screw you," Leo said. "There could be broken glass on the bottom, or sharp shells. If I cut my foot open, would you still be laughing?"

"Glass tends to get worn down quickly," Will said absently. "It doesn't stay sharp for long, especially in moving water like this. It tumbles around and wears down against rocks and sand until the edges are smooth."

"Yeah?" Leo said, carefully not looking at Will. "You've seen it?"

"Yeah. It's called 'sea glass'. I've always liked it, the way nature takes our litter, something that's dangerous, and turns it into something beautiful."

When did you see it? Where? Leo wanted to ask, but he already knew what the answer would be. Will would go quiet, then he would say, *I don't remember.*

"Come on, one more step. Doesn't the cool water feel good?"

Snorting, Leo said, "It's not like you can feel how hot it is outside."

"I have an idea of it," Will said, his tone dry. "Anyway, you were the one complaining about the heat. Let's see if you can make it to where the water's up to your waist."

"Fine." It *was* hot, an oppressive, wet heat that made even breathing feel difficult. Leo took a few more steps, wavering as the pressure on his legs increased and the ground dipped lower than he expected. He managed not to fall, and even if he had, it was still really shallow here, as Will had pointed out. He got to where the water was lapping at the bottom of his shorts, then turned back toward the shore. "I'm cooler now," he said. "Let's do something else."

"All right." There was a shadow of amusement in Will's voice, but thankfully, he didn't tease. "What should we do now?"

~

Leo had been a night owl for most of his life. Especially when he'd been a teenager on summer break, he'd gone to sleep late and lounged in bed for as long as he could get away with in the mornings—which was pretty long, since his grandma didn't care and would let him sleep in as much as he wanted. Usually it was Will who woke him, saying his name and brushing static along the back of his hand at around ten or eleven o'clock until Leo gave in and got up.

He'd learned to sleep anywhere and sleep heavily during his travels, regardless of whether he was in an uncomfortable plane seat or a noisy youth hostel, but he'd never been an early bird. Even taking jet lag into account, it was weird to wake up, peer at his phone, and realize it was only five-thirty in the morning. He blinked. For a moment, the air in front of him seemed to shimmer.

"Will?" he whispered. He blinked again and the shimmering was gone. Had he actually seen it, or was he imagining things? "Will?" he repeated, looking around wildly, but there was nothing. No wavering air, no glow, and no voice whispering back to him.

Instead he heard his new roommate moving around in the main room, quiet but definitely there.

The air was thick and warm and dry. It had gotten hotter and hotter last night despite the window being open, as though the world was wrapped in a blanket. Still, Leo hadn't expected to see Elijah in a bathing suit when he opened his door.

"Leo?" Elijah looked at him curiously as Leo's gaze darted around the room, searching for any sign of Will's shimmer before returning to Elijah. "Is something wrong?"

"No, I—No." Leo shook his head and eyed Elijah's swimsuit. "You're going to a pool?"

Elijah shook his head, his eyes curving as he smiled. "Not exactly," he said. "Why would I need a pool when the ocean is right there?" He gestured toward his front door. Leo's gaze followed the direction of his hand as though he could see through it and the intervening houses to the water beyond. Elijah cocked his head to one side. "Would you like to join me?"

"I'm not a strong swimmer," Leo demurred.

"You can stay in the shallows," Elijah said. "The tide is very high, but the water should be calm this morning." Elijah must use a lot of sunscreen, Leo thought, or else he only ever went out early or late in the day. His pale skin stood out from the shadowed room behind him, his dark eyes framed by thin wire-rimmed glasses, black hair and eyelashes, brown nipples and dark swimsuit the sole contrasting elements. His arms and torso showed an appealing, wiry strength that hadn't been evident under his clothing.

"In that case, sure. Let me just get my swimsuit," Leo said. "How often do you swim?" he tossed back over his shoulder as he went for his suitcase.

"Three, sometimes four times a week in the summer," Elijah's voice came through the slightly-open door. "Less often in winter; the water gets cold and I don't like wearing a wetsuit."

"Nice," Leo said, yanking up his swimsuit, crumpled from where he'd stuffed it between other clothes. Like Elijah's, it was a simple boxer-style. He wondered why Elijah didn't wear something sleeker if he swam regularly.

The sky was bright, but still early-morning grey as Elijah led them across the street to a path between two of the houses. It ended up at a staircase which zig-zagged down a cliffside—an actual cliff wall rather than the steep hill Leo had seen at the other beach.

The view was beautiful. In one direction a distant pier stretched out into the water. In the other, the coast disappeared into the horizon. Straight ahead as far as he could see was a wide stretch of water, as grey as the sky in the early morning light.

There was just one problem, Leo realized as he looked down. "There's no beach!"

"There usually is, it's just high tide right now," Elijah said patiently.

Leo gazed at where the water washed all the way up to the base of the cliff. "Are you sure it's safe?"

"As long as you stay in the shallow part, you should be all right," Elijah repeated. "But you don't have to come if you don't want to. I can give you the key and you can go back." He reached for a Velcroed pocket on his suit and pulled out a house key—that must have been why he wore boxer style instead of something tighter.

Leo drew a breath. The hot, oppressive air from earlier was being pushed out by a cool, salt-laden breeze. "No, I'll come." Elijah didn't respond, just replaced the key and started down the stairs.

The wooden staircase felt far more rickety than the wide concrete one Leo had seen at the other beach. It was plastered with "No Trespassing!" and "Beach Access for Residents Only" signs at every turning. "Is this a private beach?" Leo couldn't help but ask.

"What?" Elijah followed the direction of his gaze. "Oh, no. The beach itself is open to anyone coming from the north or south. But this particular access stairway is maintained by the residents of this street, so technically we can't allow others to use it. It's a liability thing."

"Ah. But I'm okay because I'm with you?"

"Yes," Elijah said. They reached the last turning before the final set of stairs down into the water and Elijah set something down on the wooden floor—a clamshell-style glasses case. Leo hadn't even noticed he'd had it in his hands. He watched as Elijah pulled off his glasses, tucked them into a hard case, snapped it closed, and left them next to the foot of one of the wide wooden posts holding up the railing.

"You're just going to leave them there?" Leo said. "What if something happens to them?"

"Like what?" Elijah said. His face was different without them, more vulnerable.

"Someone could take them, or they could blow away, or, I don't know. Get knocked into the water?"

"I have a spare set at home," Elijah said. "But I've been doing this for years and never lost a pair. The case is a heavy one, so I doubt it will blow away. This staircase doesn't get much traffic, especially at this time of day, and the glasses wouldn't do anyone much good unless they matched my prescription. And if they do match it and take them, they probably need the glasses more than I do."

"I suppose that's one way of looking at it," Leo said, but Elijah was tensing up and turning away to look at the water, his back to the staircase. Leo looked around, feeling his brows draw together.

A couple of surfers were coming up the stairs. They were a matched set, a buff guy in a wetsuit carrying a surfboard followed by an equally built woman in her own wetsuit and carrying her own board. "You did great today," she was saying. "A few more lessons and you'll be ready to try standing up."

Leo smiled at them and nodded as they went by. "Morning."

Both of them glanced at him and gave him half-smiles of acknowledgment. "Morning," said the guy, and the woman nodded back. They pressed past Leo and Elijah and headed up the narrow staircase.

"Neighbors of yours?" Leo asked.

Elijah's back was stiff and tight. He shrugged. After a moment he said. "I haven't met them, but I haven't met most of the people on my street. They're probably locals."

"You haven't met the people on your street? Haven't you lived here your whole life?"

Shrugging again, Elijah turned at last. His expression was blank. "Let's get down to the water."

"Sure," Leo said, and followed him the rest of the way down the staircase.

~

"Do you have a lot of friends?"

"Huh?" Leo looked up from his phone. He'd intended to look something up and gotten distracted replying to texts.

"Back home. Do you have a lot of friends?" Will repeated.

"I mean, I guess," Leo said uncomfortably. "I'm not, like, super popular or good at sports or anything. But I get along with people pretty well."

"You're likable," Will said.

Leo felt his face getting hot. "Uh, thanks, I guess." He frowned. "Why are you asking?"

"I'm not—I wasn't good at making friends."

"Back when you were alive, you mean?" Leo waited for Will to reply, but there was nothing, just steady silence and the faintest of shimmers. "You don't seem shy to me."

"It's different with you. It's different like this."

"As a ghost? That makes sense."

"Does it?"

"Well, I mean, you don't have to worry about anything, right? You can't get hurt and no one can see you, so it doesn't matter. Kind of nice, in a way," he said, trying to sound encouraging. Really, it had to be horribly lonely, being a ghost. "I mean, it sucks, but at least you can't do anything embarrassing."

"I can in front of you," Will said.

"Well, yeah, but you know I'm cool," Leo said, hoping he sounded confident. "You know I'm not gonna make fun of you if you say something stupid or something. Not *too* much, anyway." He forced a smile and rolled over on his side, propping his head up with one hand. "And then you can remind me of all the times that I said something stupid. It's a whole thing."

"A thing?"

"Yeah. It's what good friends do."

"Are we good friends?"

"Aren't we?" Leo stared at the shivering air. "I mean, I know it's kinda weird, but I'd say you're one of my closest friends. Maybe my best friend."

Will's voice was soft and a little strangled. *"Really?"*

"Yeah. I don't spend nearly as much time with anyone as I spend with you." He let his hand slide out from under his head and flopped back to stare at the ceiling. "In your case, you don't have a lot of options though, huh? I probably wouldn't be your first choice if you could pick anyone who could hear you."

"You would," Will said quickly. "Not at first, not before I knew you, of course. But now, I'd definitely pick you."

"Really?" Leo said, echoing Will's disbelieving tone.

"Yes," Will said firmly. "You're my best friend, too. I'd pick you every time."

~

The water was surprisingly pleasant: cool, but not nearly as cold as Leo had expected it to be. Still, it was disconcerting that the bottom of the staircase went down *into* the water itself. Leo gingerly waded in, stepping down the last stair and onto the sand with a cautious step. Elijah watched him, then walked down the last step and into the ocean as naturally as if the water wasn't even there.

"Show off," Leo muttered, and Elijah shook his head, looking like he was trying to hold back a grin.

"I've been coming to this beach my entire life," he said. "I'm just used to it."

The wide sweep of water was overwhelming. Everywhere Leo looked was either water or cliff wall, with the spindly staircase the only means to get back up. Shivering, he wrapped his arms around himself.

"If you come deeper, your body will adjust more quickly," Elijah said. He took a couple of steps further into the water, then turned and looked at Leo inquiringly.

"I'm really not a strong swimmer," Leo croaked.

Elijah's encouraging smile faded into a frown. "You don't have to do this," he said.

Gritting his teeth, Leo said, "I *want* to." That wasn't precisely true. It wasn't that he wanted to, he was just determined not to let his fear win. He'd been scared of the water for far too long. Pools didn't bother him. Anywhere that he could see the bottom easily and rely on it being relatively even and man-made, he was fine. But here...he looked around at the blue-grey water, foaming as it crashed and washed up against the cliffside again and again. There was no telling what was underneath it.

"I'll go first," Elijah said. "You can follow me." He held out his hand.

Leo blinked at the outstretched hand. Had Elijah willingly touched him, except that moment when he'd put his hand on Leo's shoulder? Leo couldn't remember.

He took the offered hand.

Slowly, Elijah led them deeper. "There's a little drop here," he said, just before stepping forward and dipping downward as though he'd gone down another invisible stair. Leo gripped his hand and followed. He could do this.

"You must be a really good swimmer," Leo said, his teeth still clenched despite himself. The water was swirling up around his knees and the sand was being pulled from beneath his feet as the water receded. They'd only gone a few steps, he told himself. He could make it deeper than this.

"My parents got me a private instructor when I was very young," Elijah said, his voice calm and steady. "Long before I met—" he stopped, then went on, "Long before I finished elementary school. Since we live so close to the water, they didn't want to have to worry about me drowning. My teacher was a professional lifeguard, so she didn't just teach me to swim. She taught me what to do if something went wrong, and how to save other people's lives."

"Th-that's awesome," Leo said, forcing himself to take another step. The waves were breaking maybe twenty feet away, washing forward each time. They tugged at Leo's legs, both on the way in and on the way back out. "Have you ever saved anyone's life?"

"Once," Elijah said. "There was a guy surfing alone. He wiped out and got whacked by his board. I was able to drag him to shore and give him mouth to mouth while a passing jogger called 911."

Squeezing Elijah's hand, Leo said, "That's amazing. How did it feel?"

"At the time it was both terrifying and—and also not. I knew what I had to do and I did it. I don't think my head has ever been so clear. Afterward, though," Elijah shuddered, "a reporter came to my door and wanted to interview me."

"You didn't want to be interviewed?" Leo thought he would have enjoyed the attention, if he'd been in Elijah's place.

"No." Elijah gave another, apparently involuntary shudder. "I just wanted to be left alone."

Pieces were starting to come together in Leo's head. Elijah's resistance to grocery shopping in-person. The way he'd turned away from the people on the stairs, people who were probably his neighbors. His evident fear and frustration at the idea of publicly being lauded as a hero.

"I'm sorry that happened," Leo said. "You shouldn't have been punished for helping someone."

Shrugging, Elijah shook his head. "Most people wouldn't have found it so upsetting. I'm just..." His silence was telling.

Weird. Strange. Broken. Leo could hear all the words he wasn't saying.

"You're not," Leo said softly.

Elijah sighed, his shoulders giving a little jerk. "Can you tread water?"

"Yes," Leo said. "That much I can manage."

"If we can get beyond the breakers the water is flat and calm. You can tread water there and relax."

Leo eyed the waves. The biggest of them were higher than his head. "Can I get past them without swimming?"

"You can just go over them," Elijah said. "Or push through them. Come on, I'll show you," he coaxed. "You can make it a little farther. Even if you don't make it all the way out, let's see if you can get to where the water's up to your waist."

...where the water's up to your waist.

It was a completely innocuous phrase, the kind of thing anyone might have said. There was nothing unique or special about it. Certainly nothing identifying.

But just like that, Leo knew. All the little things that he'd noticed without realizing he was doing so, the familiarity of the stories in the novels, the way he felt so comfortable around Elijah, especially when Elijah *spoke* –

His grip tightened on Elijah's fingers. His heartbeat, already rapid, leaped even higher. His breath stopped, then started again, coming too fast.

"...Will?" Leo's voice was high and choked.

Elijah went still. It was only for a millisecond, but Leo *felt* it, felt the jerk against his hand, saw the tightening in the muscles of Elijah's back, the way his shoulder blades pushed together as his shoulders stiffened.

Turning, Elijah met his eyes. "What?" he said, voice even, but now that Leo was looking for it, he could hear the note underneath, breathless and charged.

"You're Will." Leo *knew* he was right. He searched Elijah's – *Will's* – face, holding his gaze until Will's blank expression gave way to one of wary resignation.

Swallowing, Elijah nodded once. He didn't speak.

"You're alive," Leo whispered. "You didn't fade away or – or get exorcised or something. You're *alive*." He took one step forward, then another, stumbling a little as the water pulled at him and the sand slid under his feet. Elijah caught him as Leo threw his arms around him. "You're here. You're here."

For a long moment, Elijah stood stiff and still. Then, hesitantly, his arms came up around Leo, pulling him closer. "I'm here."

"Why didn't you tell me," Leo said into Elijah's shoulder. "Why did you lie?" He pulled back, wiping his nose on the back of his free hand.

"Let's not have this conversation here," Elijah said with a sigh. "Here, rinse your hand in the water and let's go back."

Leo just nodded and bent down to swirl his hand in the water before docilely following Elijah, hardly noticing the trip back to the stairs, up the rickety stairway, across the street, and back to the house. Elijah insisted on sluicing their feet off with a garden hose before going inside, then made Leo wait while he got a towel (Elijah's own towel was conveniently hanging just inside the door, where houses in a colder area would have had a row of jackets and scarves).

Through it all, Leo didn't speak. His thoughts were too chaotic to organize into anything coherent. It wasn't until they were inside again, sitting on the couch in their still-dry swimsuits, that he managed to latch onto anything. "You've been here all along."

"Yes," Elijah said. He got up and went to the kitchenette, filling two glasses with water before returning and pressing one into Leo's hand. Leo took an automatic sip. "I've been here all along."

"You were never a ghost," Leo said. Elijah just nodded. "Why did you lie?" Leo's voice came out too plaintive, and he winced a little.

"I didn't," Elijah said, but he dropped his eyes. "Not intentionally. I just didn't correct your false assumptions."

"All this time I thought you were *dead*! And then you weren't at the house anymore, and I thought you were gone forever!" The glass shook in Leo's hand.

"You left me alone." The words cut through Leo like a knife. He felt himself sag.

"I know. I'm sorry."

"Are you? Five years. Five years of going back every summer, checking every day, every hour, waiting, *hoping*—" Elijah choked. "After last year I finally stopped. I gave up. I couldn't—I couldn't keep going back and not finding you."

"I didn't mean to," Leo said. "If I'd known—if I'd known, I could have told you. Called you, emailed you, written you a *fucking* letter! Do you know how many times I saw something and wished I could have texted you a picture of it? Which I could have done if you'd ever told me your *cell phone number?*"

"I was going to!" Elijah's voice was tight, but with a ragged edge. "Do you remember the last thing you ever said to me? 'See you next summer!' But you never came back! So I couldn't tell you! I was going to. I was planning to. But you—" his voice dropped, "—you never came back."

"I'm sorry," Leo said again, helplessly. He found himself reaching out, his hands wrapping around Elijah's. "I'm sorry, I'm sorry, I didn't mean to." If only he'd taken time out from his busy traveling schedule to stop by his grandma's house, even once. "I won't leave you alone again."

Elijah closed his eyes and shook his head. "Don't make promises you can't keep. You want to travel, and I—I *can't.*"

"Will," Leo leaned forward, gently letting his forehead press against Elijah's. "Will, even if I leave, I'll come back. I won't leave you behind. *Will.*"

"That's not my name!" Elijah pulled back, his face twisting into a grimace. His eyes were wet. "Will was a lie! I'm not a ghost! I'm just a—a messed up person who can't even leave his house!"

Leo let his thumb trace soothingly back and forth against Elijah's hand. "Tell me," he said softly. "No more lies. Please. Tell me everything."

~

"You're quiet today," Leo said. "Something up?" He sprawled back in the grass and lifted a hand, shielding his face from the mid-afternoon sun. A lone cloud floated high above. It was shaped a bit like an upside-down rabbit.

"I'm just thinking," Will replied.

Leo waited. When Will didn't elaborate, he said, "About what?"

"You. You're graduating pretty soon, right?"

"Year after next," Leo said. The rabbit's ears were stretching as the wind tugged at the cloud, drawing them out.

"Will you be coming back here after that?"

"Here?" Leo frowned up at the glaring blue sky. The smell of fresh-cut grass was strong in his nose. "I don't know. I'll try to make it back while I'm in college between semesters, I guess."

"But you're coming back next summer?"

"That's the plan." Leo smiled wryly as the cloud became a figure skiing down a slope.

"So I'll definitely see you then?"

"Well, yeah. I mean, unless something comes up."

"Good." Will said.

~

Elijah yanked his hand away from Leo's and took a drink of his own water. For what felt like a long time, he didn't speak, staring across the room with a distant, unseeing look. Finally, when Leo was about to draw a breath and tell Elijah that it was all right, they could wait to discuss it, Elijah spoke.

"I don't—I'm not good at dealing with people," he said. "Ever since I was young, being around people makes me," he frowned and his gaze dropped as he seemed to hunt for the word he wanted, "anxious. Large groups of people are particularly difficult, especially strangers. But even being around a few people I don't know makes me uncomfortable."

Leo nodded, remembering the way Elijah had tensed up on the stairs. "Did something…happen? Something that caused you to feel that way?" he said, trying to phrase it as delicately as he could.

"No." Elijah sighed and briefly pursed his lips. "It's just been like this for me for as long as I can remember."

"School must have been hell."

"Yes, it was awful," Elijah said. "I sat in the back of the class and hid out in the library whenever I could, but I lived in fear of having the teacher call on me." His gaze went distant again, heavy with memories. "With people I know, it's easier. By the end of each year, I would be starting to get to know my classmates, at least a little, and things wouldn't be quite so bad. Then we would break for summer, and then I would go back in the fall and have to start all over again."

Fighting down the urge to reach for his hand once more, Leo said, "And during summer?"

Elijah's lips twitched. "Summers were different. When I was young, my grandpa used to look after me. He was part of the family, and something of a recluse himself, so we were fine together. But when I was ten he passed away."

"I'm sorry," murmured Leo.

Giving a nod of acknowledgement, Elijah went on, "My parents used to own a tourist trap in town, a kitschy little place that sold t-shirts and mugs. They worked there pretty much all day, every day. They knew I was fairly self-sufficient, and they definitely knew I wouldn't accept any sort of summer camp or having a stranger come to stay with me. So they left me on my own. I know some people would criticize them for that." He glanced sideways at Leo, who shrugged.

"My cousin was babysitting when she was eleven," he offered. "And you know how much freedom to wander my grandma gave me. I've never been someone who thinks that anyone under eighteen needs constant supervision."

Another nod. "Anyway, I stayed at home and read, mostly. Both books and the internet. But one day, I," he hesitated and glanced at Leo again. Leo waited. "I was lying in bed, reading, and I," Elijah wet his lips, "I started...drifting."

"Drifting?"

"I don't know how else to describe it. I thought I was dreaming at first. I'd actually managed to make a friend in school the previous year and I wondered how he was doing. And suddenly, it was like I was there, in his room, watching him. He was taking care of his younger sister, changing her diaper. I tried to talk to him, but he couldn't see or hear me."

"So, some kind of astral projection," Leo said. He wasn't as surprised as he supposed he should be. He'd been friends with a 'ghost' for years. It didn't matter if the ghost wasn't actually a ghost but a living person. Well, it *did* matter, but not because of the mechanics. "An actual out of body experience."

"I guess." Elijah finished his water, draining the glass in three quick swallows before setting it on the floor by the couch. He rested his elbows on his knees, his head hanging down. Taking a deep breath, he went on, "After that day I started, you might call it 'wandering'. Mostly around town. At first I would think about someone I knew and I would be drawn right to them. But sometimes it didn't work. I discovered that, if someone was too far away, I couldn't find them. I tried to 'visit' the lifeguard who'd taught me to swim, but nothing happened. I learned later that she'd moved to Hawai'i."

"So how did you find me?" Leo asked.

Snorting, Elijah said, "I'm getting there. I started trying to increase my range. I stopped trying to find people and started targeting places. It wasn't very precise, but if I 'visited' somewhere once, I could usually find my way back again. I ended up skipping around, randomly ending up all over. In houses, in shopping malls, in amusement parks. I saw some amazing things, and a few really bad things." He shivered. "But no matter where I went, no one could ever see me or hear me."

"Until me," Leo whispered.

"Until you." Elijah squeezed his eyes shut for a moment. Then, without looking, he reached for Leo's hand. Leo gladly gave it, interlacing their fingers. "I was testing how 'far' I could go. Distance didn't mean quite the same thing as it does when traveling for real. I mean, it didn't take me six hours to get there, not like being on an airplane. But it still mattered, because it made it harder to target specific places. So I just went wherever. One day I found myself in a small room with another boy, a little younger than myself. And he said to me, 'Are you a ghost?'"

"I—he didn't make you uncomfortable?"

Elijah shook his head. "I wasn't truly there. Being around people wasn't scary when they couldn't see or hear or touch me. Suddenly this person *could* see and hear me, sort of, but I wasn't scared. He didn't know anything about me, couldn't actually see me. He was intriguing, not frightening. So when I had to leave, I memorized how I'd gotten there so I could go back the next day."

"You didn't even tell him your real name," Leo said, his voice low.

"That wasn't entirely intentional." Elijah leaned forward slightly, moving into Leo's space. "I was going to ask you a question—I don't remember what, now, probably something like 'Will you keep it a secret if I tell you?' – but I wasn't sure if I should say anything about it at all, so I stopped before I'd finished. And you assumed it was 'Will', which was an easy solution. So I didn't contradict you."

"But you told me your real address."

"I did. You put me on the spot, and I panicked a little. Later I realized that I could have made something up. It wasn't as though you would have known the difference. I didn't like lying to you, though. I'd already told you that I couldn't remember how I died. I decided I would just keep saying that I couldn't remember anything about who I'd been. It was still a lie, but it was a simple one. But I slipped up with the address. I'd hoped you would forget all about it."

"I'm glad I didn't."

Elijah looked away. "Me too," he said.

"Are you?" Leo squeezed his hand. "You didn't tell me the truth back then, and you didn't tell me the truth when I found you again and asked if the name 'Will' meant anything to you.. Do you truly want me around?"

"Of *course* I want you around!" Elijah yanked his hand away and pressed the heels of his hands against his eyes for a moment, his back curving as he hunched forward. "Do you have any idea how it felt to look through the peephole and see you standing on my doorstep after all these years?" The curve of his back softened, drooping, his voice going quiet and resigned. "But you're just going to leave again. You'll leave and forget about me and make new friends. You'll – you'll leave me behind. And that's the way it should be. Otherwise I'll just drag you down."

"Drag me – how would you drag me down?"

The tension came rushing back. "Because I *can't deal with people,*" Elijah burst out, dropping his hands and sitting up. His eyes were red, his normally pale cheeks flushed. "All you want to do is travel, and all I can do is stay in one place!"

"Okay. Okay," Leo said, trying to breathe evenly. "First of all, I never forgot you. I – I did leave you alone, and I'm sorry for that. But I never met anyone who took your place. And I missed you. It's true, I had a lot going on and I didn't think about you every day. But every time I saw something amazing, I would wish I could share it with you."

"But you can't," Elijah said dully. "Because *I* can't."

"You can't travel. But can you still...drift?"

Elijah stiffened.

"You can, can't you? You came to my room this morning, before I woke up."

"If I can," Elijah whispered. He twisted his hands together in his lap, the color ebbing from his cheeks. "You won't—you won't tell anyone, will you?" His shoulders were stiff, but his lips were trembling.

"I won't. I swear. I swear it." It wasn't a hard promise to make. Leo had already been in the habit of secrecy about Will. He'd known it was unlikely anyone would believe him even if he tried to tell them, since he seemed to be the only person who could see or hear Will anyway. But he hadn't wanted to take the risk that someone might decide to exorcise Will, or decide that Leo was spending too much time alone talking to an 'invisible friend'. He'd made sure he had plausible deniability as much as possible, keeping his phone with him on the rare occasions that he went somewhere more public than the forest with Will.

"That was the real reason I didn't want to tell you." Elijah's eyes met his and Leo had to keep himself from reeling back at the haunted expression in them. "If anyone finds out about what I can do, I'll either spend the rest of my life in a lab or end up on TV, with everyone knowing who I am."

"That won't happen," Leo said, "because no one's going to find out."

"I never even told my *parents*," Elijah said. "It was almost like I was living two lives, like I really was a ghost named Will half the time. Then my mom and dad would get back from work a little after five o'clock—eight at night for you because of the time difference—and I would come back here and eat dinner and I would be Elijah again. I never told them about you. I never told anyone." He drew a shaky breath. "But I was going to. When you came back for the last summer before your senior year, I was going to tell you everything. But you never came back. I kept returning to the house each day, searching, but you weren't there. And then I tried to find you, but you weren't nearby. And there are thousands and thousands of people with your name. I didn't even know where to start."

A creeping restlessness pushed Leo to his feet. He paced back and forth a couple of times. "I—" he started, stopped, and started again. "I won a contest."

"A contest?" Elijah prompted after a moment.

"An art contest. The theme was, 'Why I want to Visit Japan'. I worked really hard on my entry, and...I won."

"I wish I could have seen it," Elijah said wistfully.

"I have a picture of it on my phone," Leo said. "I'll show it to you later." He flung his arm out in a slashing motion. "Not important. The thing is, the prize was to spend a month in Japan. It was a sister-city thing."

"Oh," Elijah said. His own expression went a little unfocused.

"I asked if I could do both—spend a month at grandma's *and* a month in Japan, but my parents said 'no'. That was too much. And I figured, it was a once in a lifetime experience, to win a trip to Japan, right? So I went." He stopped pacing, staring at the floor. "I'm sorry."

"No, I. No. Don't apologize. I wouldn't have wanted you to give up that opportunity for—for me," Elijah said.

Leo combed a hand back through his hair. "I thought you would probably understand. But I didn't like it. The next year I spent pretty much all summer getting ready for college. I had to go live in the dorms and my parents made me clean out my room completely. Half the summer was just hauling things to the thrift store or the dump." Shaking his head, he said, "I wanted to go to grandma's, but there just wasn't *time*."

"I understand," Elijah said.

Sighing, Leo settled back on the couch again and let his head tip back, blinking at the ceiling. It was one of those textured kinds, a 'popcorn' ceiling. Hard to clean, he thought.

"And then, I was at school. I came home for winter break. My grandma flew out to spend Christmas with us, and I kept thinking, I wished you could have come, too. She was getting frailer and my parents were talking about getting someone to stay with her and help her around the house. I went back for spring semester, and then it was summer again. And I...I really have no excuse for not coming to see you then. Grandma's carer was staying in my old room, but I could have crashed on the couch. I could have come. I should have."

"You just went home for the summer, then?" Elijah said.

"No. I, uh. I went to Greece."

"Greece!"

"I followed a bunch of travel blogs, and there was a mistake fare. A really cheap flight. I bought it, thinking they wouldn't honor it, but then they did. So I got to fly to Greece."

"I should have realized," Elijah said, fondness and bitterness warring in his voice. "I used to wonder if maybe you'd died, but you'd just found a way to live your dream."

"I should have gone back." Leo let himself look over at Will—at Elijah. "I should have tried to get back to my grandma's house. I thought about it. But I could never find a cheap fare at the right time. Sometimes when school was on they would have one, but never during the summer. Even though I flew all over the world on mistake fares and last-minute cheap tickets, I never made it back to her house. But I never forgot you."

"Leo," Elijah whispered. He turned away as his face started to crumple, tears spilling out at last. Leo reached out and pulled him into his arms.

~

"Do you think you ever went to prom?" Leo asked. Will's memory had such weird holes in it. Whenever Leo asked him anything directly, he always said he didn't know or didn't remember. But sometimes he'd talk about things he'd done or said or that had happened to him.

"I don't know," Will said like clockwork.

Leo made a face. "Of course you don't," he muttered. Will didn't respond, and guilt slowly welled up in Leo. Finally he said, "Sorry. If you don't, you don't. It's not your fault."

"What's got you in such a bad mood?" Will asked. They'd been paging through one of his grandma's photo albums, laughing at photos of his mom when she'd been a kid. Leo stared down at a grainy, faded image of her in a fancy dress standing next to a guy he'd never seen, a corsage on her wrist.

"Ahh, nothing," Leo said. "It's just, there's this guy. He's gonna be a senior next year when I'm a junior. And I thought he might, maybe," he swallowed dryly and said in a rush, "I thought he might invite me to prom next year."

Will's shimmer slid backward and hovered. "Oh?"

"Yeah. But I found out, he's already promised someone else he's gonna ask her. And I mean, that's fine. It's not like he promised me or anything. I just kinda hoped..." he turned away from Will's wavering form. "I just kinda hoped. I mean, it would have been cool to get to go with him."

No reply. Eventually Will's voice came, as low and thin as though he was fading like an old photograph. "I'm sorry."

"Nah, it's fine. I'm fine." Leo pushed himself up. "Come on. Let's see if my grandma wants us to pick some of those wild berries for her."

~

Elijah was Will. Will was Elijah. Leo yawned, opened his eyes, and stared up at the ceiling—more popcorn—letting that knowledge soak into him. He'd thought he'd left Will behind, and he had. Elijah wasn't a ghost, but he was alone. He'd been alone for a long time.

Sitting up, Leo stretched.

He'd gotten a second chance. He wasn't going to waste it. He threw off the covers and went to brush his teeth and wash his face.

By the time he'd finished and wandered into the main room, Elijah was just stepping into the house, toweling himself off. His hair was wet, his pale skin flushed with exertion.

"Did you have a good swim?" Leo said.

Nodding, Elijah finished drying himself and hung his towel by the door. Leo let himself watch, tracing over Elijah's body with hungry eyes. Elijah turned and caught him. He went still.

"Elijah," Leo said. He kept his hands at his sides, forcing himself not to pull them into fists. "Elijah," he said again. "It's true, I'm going to travel again. Not any time soon, but eventually." He held Elijah's startled gaze. "I want you to come with me."

"I can't—" Elijah started.

Holding up a hand, Leo cut him off. "Not in person. Come with me as Will."

Surprise flickered across Elijah's expression, quickly followed by comprehension. "As — as a ghost?"

"Yes. Come with me. *Can* you? I mean, if I fly somewhere, can you come with me?"

"I can," Elijah said softly. "As long as I stay with you, I can follow you anywhere. But," he dropped his eyes before lifting them again challengingly. "It's not like when we were kids," he said. "You'll be in a city, not the middle of a forest. If you talk to yourself, people are going to look at you strangely."

Snorting, Leo said, "That's the easiest thing to explain. I'll just hold my cell phone up like I'm talking to someone. Or get one of those stupid-looking headsets. Besides, I don't care what people think of me."

"I won't really be with you," Elijah said. "I won't be able to try the food with you, or smell the air, or help you if you get sick or hurt."

"I've always traveled alone before," Leo said with a shrug. "This would be better." His eyes narrowed. "And you did help me once before, didn't you? Back when I broke my leg. *You* were the one who called the ambulance."

Elijah looked sheepish. "It took me awhile to figure out how to direct them there, and which number to call. It would be even harder with you in a foreign country."

Leo rubbed the back of his neck. "It would still be better than not having anyone even knowing where I was. Though if you ever did want to come with me , maybe just a short flight, I could act as a buffer for you. You wouldn't have to talk to anyone."

"Planes aren't so bad if I know the people sitting next to me," Elijah admitted. "I flew to Hawai'i once with my parents over winter break. They let me have the window seat and didn't make me talk to anyone. I pretended to sleep whenever the stewardess came by and my parents talked to her for me. But the airports before and after — " he grimaced.

"Right, of course. Maybe a small local airport? Somewhere without long lines and without lots of people. We could come in on a red eye, arriving early or late. Go somewhere there aren't too many people, maybe the desert or some of the lesser-traveled national parks. Or you could stay in the hotel room while I see the sights. I could bring you back food to sample." Leo smiled and shrugged. "That's if you even want to try physically going somewhere. I mean, we can try to make it work. But honestly, I'd be happy just to have you with me as Will. You don't need to be there in body if you're there," his smile widened into a grin, "in spirit."

"Would it really be enough for you?" Elijah searched his eyes.

"As long as I could come back and see you in person sometimes, yeah, I think it would. I spent every summer with a ghost for years. I got used to it."

Holding his gaze, Elijah took a step forward, then another. He swallowed. "There's one other thing," he said.

"What's that?" Leo whispered.

Moving slowly, Elijah reached out and slid his hands around Will's waist. "I want to be more than a ghost to you. I want—" His breath caught on the words. "I want—"

"Yeah," Leo said, the word raw in his ears. "Me too." He closed the distance between them.

He'd thought about kissing Will once or twice. But how could you kiss someone without lips? The fantasies had always been vague and formless, dreamy late-night thoughts more than full-blown lusty visions.

Now that he knew Will was Elijah, the nebulous attraction he'd felt for his friend transformed into something much deeper and wider. He'd already been drawn to Elijah before he'd realized the truth, and once he did, it pulled him under with the power of a wave, terrifying and exciting.

"W— Elijah," he whispered. Elijah's kiss was clumsy and inexperienced. Leo smiled against his lips and said, "Like this." He let his mouth go soft against Elijah's, his tongue resting lightly against Elijah's lower lip. Elijah shuddered and pressed forward, but Leo pulled back. "Slowly," he said. "I'm not going anywhere."

"Leo," Elijah breathed. His hands tightened on Leo's waist, and Leo leaned in again, teasing.

"You've been waiting a long time, haven't you?" he breathed into Elijah's ear.

"So long." The words came out as a gasp. "*Leo.*"

"I'm here." He ran a soothing hand up Elijah's spine to cup the back of his neck. "I'm here."

~

"They're beautiful," Leo murmured, craning his neck. "So *big*."

The air shimmered off the desert sand. He didn't turn to look at his companion, just smiled and said softly, "I can't believe we finally made it here."

"Is it everything you imagined?"

"So much more," Leo said. "It's always like that, seeing things like this." He gazed at the Great Pyramid of Giza, his chest tight with awe. "What about you?"

"Yes." The voice was a whisper on the wind.

"Yes?"

"Yes. It's better than I imagined."

Leo's fingers twitched and he felt a touch on the back of his hand. "The pyramids?" he said hoarsely.

"Being here with you."

He couldn't help but smile at that. His love was such a romantic. "Any idea of what you want to write?"

"A few things. Any idea of what you want to draw?" Elijah said, echoing back his words with an added note of challenge.

"Oh, lots," Leo said. "It's difficult to capture the *scale* of it, though. Maybe I'll try to render what it might have looked like with the original limestone layer on top."

Neither Elijah's travel writing nor Leo's art had had much success on their own, but it turned out that when presented together as a unit, they were surprisingly popular. Elijah was still writing novels, off and on, but they had a growing fanbase following them online, eager to see each new image and accompanying words—usually a discussion of the trip itself, but sometimes including a short story, original poem, or scholarly discussion of the history of the place.

"Our online donations are already enough to pay for our next trip," Leo said. "And did I tell you? I got a call from an actual travel magazine."

"You mentioned it," Elijah said, "a few times."

"Sorry. I'm just excited," Leo said. He let his arm swing out slightly, brushing against Elijah again. "Next week," Leo added, knowing Elijah would understand.

"Next week," Elijah agreed. "You're still sure about this?"

"Very sure. Completely and utterly sure," Leo said. "Why? You're not getting cold feet, are you?"

"No! Of course not. There's nothing I want more."

"Good. Then it's settled." Next week, Leo would return home, back to the house next to the ocean that he and Elijah shared. And then, the two of them were going to elope. Not far, just to the local courthouse, where Leo had already made arrangements in advance such that they wouldn't have to wait in line or end up in a crowd.

Their honeymoon wouldn't exactly be conventional. A week spent at home, just the two of them, and then Leo would be leaving again while Elijah stayed behind. Except that Elijah would be with him in all the ways that mattered most. Leo would describe the food he tried and complain about the humidity, and Elijah would turn his words and the sights they saw together into something beautiful. Leo would put pen or brush to paper and paint a vivid scene or draw an amusing cartoon to go with them. And then they would be able to do it again.

"We make a good team," Leo said fondly. Elijah didn't respond, but Leo felt a tingling brush of static against his cheek and another against his lips, stealth kisses. Laughing, he adjusted his headset and took out his sketchbook.

A Touch of Magic

There was a naked man in the middle of the room. Why was there a naked man in the middle of the room?

Lawrence blinked and pulled his eyes away, taking in the students standing in a wide, loose ring, each with an easel in front of them.

Right. This was the art department. The guy was a model. Right. It wasn't weird. The guy was supposed to be here. He was *supposed* to be naked.

"Can I help you?" came a sharp voice. Relieved at the distraction, Lawrence met the speaker's eyes. Ah. This must be the teacher. He was clearly older than everyone else in the class (including the model, who looked to be about the same age as the students).

"Uh, sorry. Didn't mean to interrupt." Lawrence straightened his back and drew in a breath. "I'm supposed to be at Theresa Marlon's class at three o'clock. For, uh, 'motion studies'." He spoke the last two words as though quoting a foreign language.

The teacher's light grey eyes held Lawrence's with a penetrating gaze. After a moment, he gave a nod and some of the tightness melted from his face. "She's on the other side of the building. Down the hall and—actually, it's probably best if I show you. Can you wait five minutes?"

Lawrence looked around for the clock and found it high on the wall. He still had ten minutes before he had to be there. "If it's really five minutes," he said. He knew all too well how a class could get dragged out by students with complicated questions. He'd been eager to leave at that age, either to get to his next class or to freedom. But there were always a handful that seemed to want to stay behind. He refused to put up with it from the classes he taught—when class was over, it was over.

The teacher didn't seem offended. He gave Lawrence a small, rueful smile and nodded. "I'll show you a shortcut; it won't take more than three to get you there." Lawrence gave him a nod in return and leaned against the back wall.

"All right, that's it for today," the teacher said. "Start cleaning up. Thank you, Brandon." The naked man shifted out of his casual sprawl and stretched. A silver ring glinted from one nipple. The edge of a tattoo curled around his leg, perhaps a dragon. Lawrence looked away again, feeling his face heat.

The room was spacious, light and airy. His own domain was the gym, with fluorescent lights and high ceilings, the smells of rubber and sweat. He was vaguely aware of the rest of the campus, of the huge classrooms like giant funnels with the teacher standing at the bottom. He hadn't known anywhere like this room existed on the grounds. It reminded him of classrooms of his youth, one entire wall taken up with windows, some so high up that they required a pole to open and close.

Despite himself his eyes wandered back to the center of the room. He was relieved to see that the model was pulling on a robe.

"Any questions before I let you go for the weekend?" asked the teacher.

A hand shot into the air, a tallish kid with his blond hair shaved into an undercut. "About imbuing," he said, and there were some exasperated noises from other students. A couple of them started packing up their things faster. "Is it true that only an expert can imbue something?"

"Not at all," the teacher said. He was doing something with his own brushes as he spoke. "It's true that many things that have been imbued were created by experts, but there have also been cases where people with no knowledge whatsoever have imbued something or someone."

Lawrence prepared to tune the man out. Imbued art had never held much interest for him.

Far more interesting were stories of people who'd managed to imbue other people. The story of the man who'd stabbed a hated mortal enemy and left behind a curse that caused her to bleed out, the wound refusing to close or heal even with modern medical intervention. Or the old story of a soldier who'd healed his lover in the middle of a battlefield (only to later be tried and executed for being homosexual). That one always made Lawrence tear up.

"As far as anyone has been able to tell, all that it takes to imbue something is pure emotion," the teacher said. He watched the class from behind his glasses, his expression serene. "But it is true that a high proportion of those who imbue something in their lifetime are experts in their field. Why do you think that might be?"

The class was shifting impatiently, packing away supplies and slinging backpacks over shoulders. Lawrence tried not to look at any of the canvases, each a different angle of the same nude figure. He narrowed his focus to the teacher instead.

"Maybe an expert is more likely to feel emotional about their work?" suggested the boy who'd spoken up initially, his tone uncertain.

The teacher shook his head. "Quite the opposite, by all accounts. The people who've imbued something have universally said that they weren't thinking about their work at all. They were only *feeling*, and the feeling was usually not directly related to what they were doing." He cocked his head and looked around the class, reminding Lawrence of a curious bird. A sparrow, maybe, or a robin. The red smock he wore over his dark brown sweater reinforced the impression. "Which may be a clue to why experts have a higher proportion of imbued creations. If you're anything less than an expert, can you afford to take your mind off what you're doing? Say you're cooking breakfast, won't you be thinking about making sure the pan is the right temperature, the eggs are beaten for the right amount of time, the proportions of ingredients are correct? Only an expert would have the luxury of *feeling*, rather than thinking, as they create."

Lawrence vaguely recalled that there'd been a few cases of chefs creating imbued dishes, though he was pretty sure it had never happened during a competition. That made sense. As a competitor himself, Lawrence knew that no matter how focused one was on the match, or how much one prepared in advance, it was incredibly difficult to just let go and allow one's body and training to take over. If there was anything at stake, it was impossible to completely forget that fact.

"Or it may simply be a function of quantity," the art teacher went on as he pulled his smock over his head, briefly muffling his voice. "If one makes thousands of paintings in one's lifetime, wouldn't that increase the chance that one of them might be imbued?" Most of the students were congregating by the door. Glancing at the clock, the teacher gave a nod and said, "Class dismissed. See you next week." The gaggle of students headed out the door with alacrity. Their teacher trailed behind until he was abreast of Lawrence.

Glancing at the clock, Lawrence said, "You made it."

"Made it?" the teacher said, blinking up at him. He was shorter than Lawrence had realized, only coming up to his chest. It must be hard, being shorter than all the guys and the majority of the girls — Lawrence caught himself and conscientiously rephrased the thought. It must be hard, being shorter than almost all of the people of any gender in his class.

"You finished the class in five minutes," Lawrence said, "even with that question at the end."

"Oh. Yes. Well, this isn't my first rodeo," the short man sniffed. "I'm Sean, by the way." He held out his hand. Lawrence shook it. He'd never thought his own hands were particularly large, but they felt like paws compared to Sean's. He gave a brief, politely firm shake.

"Lawrence Carmichael," Lawrence replied. "How long have you been teaching?" he asked as Sean led him out of the room.

"Ten years," Sean said. "You?"

"Only two," Lawrence admitted. "I'm the fencing coach."

"Oh. Oh! Lawrence *Carmichael!*" Sean said. "I've seen some of your matches!"

"Yeah?" Lawrence tried not to sound skeptical. People tended to exaggerate such things. If Sean had seen any of his matches, it had probably only been the bout where Lawrence had taken the gold.

"I fenced a bit when I was younger," Sean said diffidently. Perhaps he was a fan after all. "Before—" There was a pause as though from a caught back breath, "before I became a teacher."

Lawrence wondered what he'd been about to say. He searched for the right words to ask more about Sean's fencing experience — should he ask who he'd studied under? Why he'd stopped?

Before he could come up with a suitable question, Sean said,

"How did Theresa get you to agree to be her model, anyway? I admit I'm a little jealous."

"She offered to paint something for me," Lawrence said with a shrug. "And she's an old friend from college, so." He paused, a terrible thought striking him. "I won't have to be naked, will I?"

Chuckling, Sean shook his head. "Not for motion studies." His eyes went unfocused. "I wonder if she'd be amenable to a joint class?" he muttered as he stopped in front of a door at the end of the hallway. "Or perhaps you'd be willing to pose for my class sometime? I could paint your portrait in exchange."

"My portrait?"

"Sure, why not?"

"What would I do with a portrait of myself?"

"Give it to your boyfriend," Sean shot back.

That was interesting. It was common enough knowledge that Lawrence was gay. One didn't get to have a private life if one was a professional athlete, not at the level that Lawrence competed at. But fencing was also pretty niche. Lawrence had met plenty of people who'd claimed to be fans but who'd had no idea that he swung that way. "Don't have one right now."

Sean blew out a breath. "Fine. Give it to your mother."

Actually, that wasn't a bad idea. His mom would love to have a portrait of him. "You any good?"

The sharp reply seemed to take Sean aback. He gave a small crack of laughter and said, "You'll have to tell me." He lifted his hand to push the door open. Before he could touch it, it swung inward, making both of them jump and the person on the other side flinch and stop short when she nearly ran into them.

"Oh," Theresa said. "*There* you are."

~

The campus coffee shop was surprisingly comfortable. The coffee wasn't particularly good, though they'd tried to keep up with the trends, offering mediocre 'lattes' and halfway-decent 'cold brew' and bittersweet 'acai smoothies'.

Their pastries were mostly pre-packaged, but they did bake a few batches of muffins throughout the day, always at random, unpredictable times.

What the place lacked in overall quality it made up for in comfort. The furniture was a haphazard assortment of second-hand pieces, probably repurposed from stuff left behind when students moved out of their dorms. There were couches along the walls, a couple of mismatched stuffed armchairs, and every kind of kitchen chair and stool and small table imaginable. Rather than cluttering the space, they somehow worked together harmoniously.

There were, as always, students tucked into the armchairs. They were surrounded by empty cups and papers and looked as though they'd been there since the previous night.

Lawrence ignored them and headed for the table he'd mentally dubbed 'theirs'. Before meeting Sean, he hadn't even known about this place. But after their first motion studies session, Sean had offered to buy him coffee, and it became something of a weekly tradition after that. Sean always chose this particular table despite the fact that it was almost comically high for him, coming nearly up to his shoulder. There were no stools or chairs tall enough to reach it, so the students tended to avoid it, not wanting a 'standing only' spot.

"The thing is," Sean said one Tuesday afternoon, waving a hand and coming dangerously close to upsetting his iced tea, "imbuing is almost impossible to recreate in laboratory conditions."

Lawrence nodded, taking a sip of his cold brew and carefully moving the tea out of danger.

"How can you create a condition where someone experiences pure and untainted emotion when they *know* they're being watched? Even if they don't know what they're there for, the very knowledge that they're participating in a study is going to introduce distractions."

"So they've never gotten it to work in a lab?"

"A bare handful of times," Sean said, waving his hand again, "and only once when that was what they were *trying* to do. The other two happened by accident when they were testing something else."

"Really?" Lawrence broke his muffin in half and spread a napkin under one of the pieces before sliding it across the table to his companion.

Sean eyed the muffin half hungrily. "I shouldn't," he said with a sigh. "I'm visiting my sister later. She'll worry if I have no appetite."

"Save it," Lawrence said. "You can have it for breakfast." Sean happily wrapped up his half in the napkin and made it disappear somewhere into one of the many pockets of his voluminous shoulder portfolio bag. Lawrence had asked him once if he wasn't worried about getting crumbs on his work, but apparently the different pockets were sealed off from each other.

"Thank you," Sean said. "What was I talking about?"

"Imbuing," Lawrence said. "Making it happen under controlled conditions."

"Right!" Sean lit up as he returned to his favorite subject. Or perhaps his second favorite subject, with art being the first. It would be a close race, Lawrence reflected before his attention was drawn back to Sean's animated face. "They've tried having people watch things that are supposed to give them strong emotional reactions. They've tried giving them drugs, and tried stimulating different parts of the brain. But nothing's ever worked consistently. Most of the time, nothing's worked at all." There was a certain satisfaction in his tone. The very unrepeatability of imbuing must be fascinating to an artist.

When he'd been in elementary school, Lawrence had once seen an imbued painting on a field trip to a local museum. It was lauded as the prize of the collection: a violent mess of color that swirled and writhed disturbingly. He remembered the way his heart had pounded and the breath had felt hot in his lungs. The image and the rage it had inspired had haunted him for months afterward. He'd never seen another imbued piece until he'd been an adult and a teammate had dragged him to the Louvre when they'd been in Paris for a tournament. Seeing the Mona Lisa had been an entirely different experience. As he'd watched the way her eyes brightened and her lips twitched, trembling on the verge of a true smile before fading, he'd felt his heart soar like a helium balloon.

Still, "It's just like the videos and gifs," he'd told his teammate. She'd rolled her eyes and shaken her head at him.

"Isn't it different in person?" she'd demanded.

It had been, but he had better things to do than get pulled along on future museum trips, so he'd just shrugged.

How his teammate would laugh if she could see him now, hanging on Sean's every word. Sean just had a way of talking about it that made it immediate. Maybe it was because he was a teacher.

Or maybe it was because, Lawrence admitted to himself, it wasn't just the imbuing he was interested in.

~

Lawrence hurried across the campus at a brisk walk, once again cursing the designers for putting the art buildings at the opposite end of the grounds from the gym. It had probably been a reasonable enough decision at the time, but it sure made it hard to get to Sean's class before it was over every Tuesday and Thursday afternoon.

He made it to the art building and stopped outside room 205, taking a moment to catch his breath and sweep the loose strands of hair that had escaped his ponytail behind his ears before silently turning the knob and slipping into the back of the room.

The students, used to his presence by now, didn't even look up from their easels, standing in a loose half-circle around a dais where a nude model lay casually sprawled. A woman today, Lawrence noted vaguely, with dyed magenta hair. Was she one of the regulars? Lawrence thought she seemed familiar, but his attention was drawn like a magnet to the man at the front of the room.

"That's all for today," Sean said. "You can start cleaning up."

The rustling susurrus of students released from class began, a combination of conversations, the rattling of brushes, and the sound of water running. It varied slightly depending on what medium the class was working with that week, yet was largely identical no matter what class one was in. Lawrence's own classes were much the same, only replacing parts of it with the clank of equipment being stowed, zippers being pulled, and lockers slamming.

Strolling to the front of the room, Lawrence dodged easily around the students who were already making their way to the door. He came around and stopped at the edge of the small platform to wait. Sean would wait to use the sink to clean his own brushes until the rest of his students were finished, Lawrence knew. Glancing over his shoulder, Sean looked up at Lawrence—even elevated by the platform he was still shorter than Lawrence by a good three inches – and said, "What do you think?"

Lawrence shrugged. "Looks fine," he said. The magenta of the woman's hair stood out, eye-catching against the white background. Lawrence studied the painting Sean had been working on, his eyes involuntarily darting to the model, but she'd already risen and slipped on a robe.

"'Fine'," muttered Sean. "Do you know any other adjectives?"

A smile tugged at the corner of Lawrence's mouth. "Good?"

"So very articulate," Sean said with a put-upon sigh, but his lips twitched as well.

"I'm no artist," Lawrence said. He examined the work for another long moment before saying, "Her hair's really bright."

"Hmm." Sean tilted his head to one side and nodded. "Good eye." Picking up his brush, he tapped it in a dab of color before making three thin, sweeping lines. "There. How's that?"

"Better," Lawrence said. It never failed to fill him with awe when Sean did that, transforming the entire look of a work with a few tiny changes. In this case, the hair no longer stood out in a way that seemed unnatural, but now became part of the whole, pulling the image together. "You didn't change the color of her hair at all," he noted.

"I changed the shadows."

Lawrence nodded as though he knew what that meant. Sean smiled up at him. "Let me just clean my brushes and we can go."

The rest of the students had filed out, leaving the classroom both peaceful and slightly bereft, as empty classrooms always were. Lawrence watched as Sean cleaned his brushes and stowed them away, removed his smock, and said, "Ready."

~

When Lawrence finally went to sit for his portrait, he was struck by how bright Sean's apartment was. The front room that served as a combined dining/kitchen/living room faced east, letting in the morning light.

"Thank you for coming over early on a Saturday," Sean said,

handing him a cup of coffee. It smelled better than the campus cafe's cold brew.

"It's not that early," Lawrence said. It was true that he generally slept until eight on weekends, but that had still given him plenty of time to get there by nine. He took a sip from the mug. "This is really good."

Sean beamed.

Usually, the diminutive art teacher wore sweaters with the sleeves pushed up—soft looking ones in dark colors like brown, blue, or grey. They fit his small form well enough that he didn't swim in them. Lawrence had always figured he either bought them in the teenager section, or that he knew a really good tailor or knitter.

Today, Sean wore a t-shirt. Like the sweaters, it fit him so well that Lawrence wondered if he'd had it professionally altered. Though he was used to seeing Sean's pale forearms stained with paint and wrists that Lawrence could only think of as 'dainty' despite knowing how much Sean would dislike the description, the dark t-shirt revealed a lot more skin. It had a cheerful picture of some cartoon character on it that Lawrence didn't recognize, and both it and the faded jeans Sean wore were covered in dots and spatters and smears of paint.

"Have a seat," Sean said, indicating a comfortable looking armchair across from the window. The easel stood at an angle in front of it, tubes of paint laid out on a small table nearby. The floor looked like polished wood but was probably some sort of laminate, Lawrence thought. A rubber mat sat under the easel.

Sean's feet were bare.

"Can I get you anything else?" Sean said. "Did you have time for breakfast?"

"I ate before I came," Lawrence said, too gruffly.

But Sean didn't seem offended. He just nodded and said, "Good, good. Then when you're ready, we'll get started."

Lawrence nodded and took another drink of his coffee. There was a quote on the mug. He turned it in his hand to read the whole thing:

If I could say it in words, there would be no reason to paint.

—Edward Hopper

"It was a gift from one of my students," Sean said fondly.

"Ah." Lawrence had received a total of one gift from a student so far. It had been deeply embarrassing, with the student blushing and stammering her way through her presentation of it. He'd accepted the hand-embroidered towel and thanked her. He was glad he'd at least managed to bite back his first response, which was that it was a useless gift. Lawrence went through lots of rags and towels, and he did not treat them gently. A hand-embroidered item would either be destroyed in the course of his normal usage, or have to be carefully preserved and never used at all.

He wondered what Sean did when presented with such ridiculous tokens. Probably smiled his beautiful smile and thanked the gifter with grace. *Thank you,* Lawrence could imagine him saying with sincerity upon receiving any gift, no matter how ill-suited, *I'll treasure it.*

At the same time, Lawrence had no doubt that any student hopeful of conveying their feelings to him had been disappointed by his lack of response. It wasn't just a deliberately cultivated front where his students were concerned, either. Lawrence was fairly sure that Sean had a blind spot where he himself was concerned; the occasional, casual comment revealed that he considered himself unattractive and that he was resigned to remaining single.

It made no sense. Sure, he was small, but Sean was thoughtful and interesting and kind. Anyone would be lucky to date him.

"I'll just be doing preliminary work today," Sean said.

"That's fine," Lawrence said. "How do you want me?"

"Just like that is good," Sean said. He opened one of the tubes and put a daub of paint on the tray before picking up a brush and beginning to make quick, sweeping gestures. "Can I ask you a question?"

Anything. "Sure."

"Why the ponytail?"

"Ah." Lawrence couldn't stop his lips from quirking up. "It's not nearly as interesting as everyone makes it out to be."

"I promise I won't be disappointed," Sean said, his eyes crinkling at the corners. His arm never stopped its movements.

"I started training when I was really young," Lawrence said. "I always kept my hair short. It's a lot easier when you have to wear a full fencing mask all the time, and the last thing you want when you're competing is to leave something trailing that can distract you or catch on something. Not to mention, if your hair obscures your name on the back of your fencing jacket, in some competitions you can get a yellow card."

Nodding, Sean set down his brush and picked up a different one. His eyes darted between Lawrence's face and the easel as he worked.

"About five—no, six—no, it's been *seven* years ago now, I got injured."

"I remember," Sean said softly.

It hadn't had anything to do with fencing, just a stupid slip and fall. A bad break in his leg had required several surgeries and months and months of recovery. "I thought my career was over," Lawrence admitted. "I was certain I would never fence professionally again. So I...just stopped caring. Let my hair grow out, because what did it *matter?*"

The agony of that year, the bitter regret, the recriminations, both of himself and others, still ached after all this time.

"I'm sorry to bring up bad memories," Sean said softly.

"It's fine," Lawrence said. He cleared his throat. "Anyway, after the physical therapy and all that, when I did start getting back into fencing, everyone expected me to cut my hair. And I kept meaning to, because like I said, long hair is kind of a pain."

Sean, whose own hair was short and brown and curly, grinned. "I've had more than one student complain after getting paint in their hair."

"Exactly. But I kept putting it off, and, even though it's a pain, the longer it got, the less I wanted to cut it."

"Because it had taken you so long to grow out?" Sean tapped the end of his brush distractingly against his lips.

"Hm? Oh. Yes, partly, but also because people kept asking me about it. The more I got back into competition, the more people wanted to interview me. And every damn time, they asked about my hair. As if it mattered!"

A huff of laughter. Sean lifted his brush and shook his head. "That's very *you*, my friend."

Warmth stole through Lawrence's chest at being called Sean's friend. "Well, finally I just said, 'I'm not going to' or something like that. And then everyone made a big deal about that. What did it mean, that I wasn't cutting my damn hair? Why wasn't I cutting it? Was it in solidarity with female fencers who chose not to cut their hair? Was it in protest of something? Was it a way to remind myself of my injury, so that I wouldn't forget what I'd had to overcome?" He rolled his eyes and snorted.

Sean's full-throated laugh in response felt like a victory. Lawrence wasn't sure why; it wasn't as though Sean didn't laugh when the occasion demanded it. But something about his unrestrained shout of mirth sent a spike of pleasure and satisfaction through Lawrence.

"So, that's why," Lawrence finished.

"Out of spite," Sean said, still chuckling.

"Pretty much."

"Does it get in your way?"

"Not now that I know how to manage it," Lawrence said. "I asked some long-haired fencers I knew for tips, and they showed me how to gather it so that it wouldn't be too much of a problem. Since it's straight, it's a lot easier to manage than wavy or curly hair." Sean nodded. "Do you…" Lawrence watched as Sean's brush hesitated in its movements, waiting for him to finish his question, "do you think I should cut it?"

"What? No, I like it. That is," Sean flushed and focused on the paper in front of him, "you should do whatever makes you comfortable. If you want to cut it, don't let what anyone thinks stop you. I used to—I've seen pictures of what you looked like before you grew it out, and you're handsome either way. But I think it suits you."

The room felt hot. It must be the sun streaming through the window, Lawrence thought. "Thanks." He sounded too gruff again to his own ears, but again Sean didn't seem to mind.

~

A delicious, nutty smell was wafting from the kitchen at the back of the shop, giving Lawrence a good feeling about his chance of being able to snag a couple of muffins. He was trying not to think about the printed papers folded and tucked into his pocket.

"Good afternoon." Sean set his portfolio down next to the table and smiled up at Lawrence. Lawrence's heart tightened at how warm and open the expression was. Did he really want to risk losing this? "Afternoon," he said. "My turn to buy."

Sean's eyebrows drew together. "It is not."

"It is." Before Sean could argue anymore, Lawrence turned on his heel and strode over to where the line was forming. Hopefully he'd timed it right; too early and the muffins wouldn't be out of the oven yet, too late and they'd be gone before he made it to the front.

He shoved his sweaty hands in his pockets, then pulled them out again before they could dampen the folded papers.

When he got to the front of the line he was in luck. There were three muffins left. He glanced at the line behind him and only ordered one, as well as Sean's usual herbal tea (iced, since the weather was already edging toward summer) and his own cold brew.

When he returned to the table, Sean smiled to see the muffin. Lawrence would have offered the whole thing to him if he thought Sean would accept it. Instead, he broke it in half as usual, pushing the larger half to Sean's side of the table.

"It was definitely my turn," Sean said, even as he accepted the muffin eagerly.

"You can pay the next two times," Lawrence said. He didn't intend to allow Sean to do any such thing, but it wasn't worth arguing about right now, especially when he had something else he wanted to discuss. He cleared his throat.

Sean's eyes snapped to him. Lawrence opened his mouth. "You, uh." God, this was hard. He was an adult, a gold medalist, a well-paid coach and teacher. His face was in magazines advertising high-end clothes and watches, for heaven's sake! And yet, somehow none of that made this any easier. "You talked about that concert," he said. "The one where they're playing the imbued piece at the end?"

Nodding, Sean took a drink of his iced tea. "It sounds like it's going to be lovely. The imbued piece will be interesting, but that's not the only draw." Before Sean could continue, Lawrence reached into his pocket and shoved the printed tickets across the table. Sean took the slightly wrinkled papers, nonplussed, and unfolded them. His eyes widened. "You managed to get tickets? These are good seats, Lawrence! You're going to have a wonderful time!"

The seats hadn't been cheap, but Lawrence had pulled a few strings, or rather, his publicist had. "I wondered if," the back of Lawrence's neck was tight, "you'd like to join me."

Sean's lips parted in obvious surprise. He looked utterly stunned, his ears turning red. "*Me?*" He looked down at the tickets, then back up at Lawrence. "As a friend? Or—" He cut himself off, the blush spilling into his cheeks. "Of course as a friend, what am I think—?" he started, but Lawrence interrupted.

"As a date."

If he hadn't been so nervous, seeing Sean caught so completely off guard would have been a little funny. He looked like he'd been hit over the head. "R-really?" He looked down at the tickets, his eyes skimming them. For a heart-stopping moment, he frowned. Then he raised his head again and said, "Are you sure? There are a lot of people who would jump at the chance to go out with you."

To go out with **you**, Lawrence noted the phrasing, not *to attend this concert*. As though Lawrence himself was the draw, rather than the expensive tickets. That was a good sign. "I'm sure," he said. "I want to go with you."

"I—of course," Sean said, his already flushed face darkening even more. Lawrence had never seen him so flustered. But was he flustered because he liked Lawrence, or because he didn't know how to tell him he didn't want to go? "Of course I'll go with you, I would love to."

"Okay," Lawrence said. He reached for the tickets. "It's in two weeks. I can pick you up." Sean didn't own a car, mostly taking the subway.

"Why don't we meet at your place?" Sean said. "It's closer. We can leave from there."

"Sure." Lawrence wondered that he didn't feel any calmer. He was happy, he thought? Relieved that Sean said yes. Maybe it would hit him later. A thought struck him, sending a little jolt of panic through him. "I didn't plan for dinner or anything," he blurted out.

"That's fine," Sean said quickly. "This is, wow, more than enough. This is amazing. Thank you so much, Lawrence. I—I'm really looking forward to it." His smile was awkward but sweet. Lawrence felt his heart leap a little, as it so often did around Sean. Excitement fizzed in his chest, pushing aside the nervousness at last. He'd done it. He'd asked Sean out, and Sean had said 'yes'!

"Me too."

~

"Are there any questions?" Sean looked around the room and nodded at a red-haired student. "Bobby?"

"Do you think that imbuing is the work of God?" The student leaned forward slightly as though anticipating the answer.

"I couldn't say," Sean said. Bobby's shoulders slumped. Sean's gaze drifted back to his own canvas before returning to the student. "Throughout history, many have argued that imbuing is evidence of the existence of a higher power, of course, and claimed that imbuing is miraculous in nature."

"But what do *you* believe?" Bobby pressed.

"I'm not going to answer that," Sean said calmly. "I will say only that not all cases of imbuing have been positive. People are as likely to curse someone to a lingering, painful death as they are to cure someone of an incurable illness." His mouth twisted slightly. "Perhaps moreso. Many, many people want to cure their loved ones. Many feel like failures for being unable to do so. Yet it's that very desire that seems to get in their way, robbing the emotion of its purity." He gave his head a shake. "If it is a gift bestowed by the Almighty, it seems a cruel one. Those who most seek it cannot have it, while those who do not ask for it are given it, whether they want it or not."

"God works in mysterious ways," Bobby intoned. Lawrence did his best not to snort. The student had missed Sean's point entirely.

Making a small 'hmm' sound that neither indicated agreement nor disagreement, Sean asked, "Where do you stand on imbued murders? Should the killer be prosecuted for something that they perhaps could not help?"

Frowning, Bobby fiddled with something on a chain around his neck. Lawrence thought it was probably a cross. "If they're responsible for someone's death, of course they should," the student said.

"But *are* they responsible?" Sean let his eyes sweep over the class.

"Such cases are caused by a deep hatred, but is hatred alone enough to justify trying someone for manslaughter?"

The class shifted uncomfortably. No one responded.

"I'm not in a position to give an opinion on whether or not imbuing is miraculous," Sean went on, pacing to the left, then back to the right. "Yet I find myself loath to remove the human element. Every known case of imbuing was apparently driven by extreme emotion. It is a uniquely human phenomenon—there are no known cases of animals imbuing anything or anyone. And it is rare among humans because the situation must be exactly right for it to occur. We've all experienced intense emotions at one time or another, but to imbue something, a person must not only feel the emotion, they must be doing something at that exact moment that can channel that emotion. If anything is miraculous, I'd say it's the *ability* to imbue, not the individual cases of imbuing."

"Oh." Bobby's eyebrows furrowed. "But—"

"I'm sorry, class is over," Sean interrupted. "You'll need to save any other questions for next time."

The student left, still frowning thoughtfully. The rest of the class shuffled or hurried out. Lawrence stepped forward once they were all gone, the door closed behind them. "Do you?"

"Do I what?"

"Do you think imbuing is miraculous? I get why you can't say it in front of the students, but I'd like to know, if you're willing to tell me."

"Ah, well." Sean gave his head another little shake. "Not really. It's *too* grounded in humanity: human loves, human hates. I don't particularly believe in a higher power anyway. There are too many to choose from, and none of them seem to have a monopoly on truth. But if I did, I would find it hard to believe that any god would imbue things on a—a case by case basis, as it were. At most, it's an inherent ability of humans. And if that's so, it need not be miraculous at all, wouldn't you say?"

"I agree." Lawrence didn't believe in a higher power either, though he suspected that his and Sean's paths to that conclusion had been different. "Ready?"

"Yes, let me just get a few things." Sean hurriedly snatched up the rolled cloth with pockets for his pencils and a sketchpad. "Right. Let's get to Theresa's class. I wouldn't want you to be late again."

"It wasn't my fault we were late last time," Lawrence pointed out, carefully ignoring the fact that he didn't *have* to wait around for Sean to walk him there.

"I know, I know."

"I wasn't the one talking my students' ears off about imbuing for the last five minutes."

"Yes, yes, you're a model of restraint," Sean said dryly.

~

Lawrence handed the paper bag to Sean. Sean accepted it and peeked inside. "Croissants?"

"There's a bakery on the way," Lawrence said. "They smelled good."

"They do." Sean's face crinkled into a soft smile. It was Lawrence's favorite expression, at least when it was directed at him. "I have some coffee brewing. Shall we split one of these before we start? Or did you want a whole one?"

"A half is good," Lawrence said.

Crossing to the kitchenette at the side of the open-plan room, Sean poured two cups of coffee, holding one out to Lawrence when he followed Sean in. "Here you are. Let me get you a plate."

The easel was set up once more, assuming it had ever been taken down. The tall table next to it had tubes of paint carefully lined up next to a palette. Other than the armchair, which was still sitting across from the window, there were no other tables or chairs. Sean didn't seem bothered by the lack, handing Lawrence a saucer with half a croissant on it before casually leaning against the kitchen counter and sipping his coffee.

"Feel free to have a seat if you like," Sean said. Instead, Lawrence propped himself against the counter next to Sean and let his eyes drift around the room.

There was one bookshelf on the wall opposite the windows, stuffed with a haphazard array of hardcovers and paperbacks that seemed out of place in the otherwise neat and spare apartment. A new, framed piece of art that Lawrence didn't recognize hung next to it, a woman and child at a beach. The wind seemed to catch at her floppy hat and white dress, while the child played happily in the sand. If there was a TV in the room, Lawrence couldn't find it.

"Is the painting a print?" he asked.

"Painting? Oh, that one? No, that's one of mine," Sean said. He sighed. "I acquired it recently, but I think I'm going to take it down."

"Take it down? Why?" Lawrence looked at it with new eyes. He wondered who the woman and child were. They didn't look like Sean.

"Oh, you know how it is," Sean said fretfully. "I used to be proud of it, but as I've improved, it's hard to see anything but my mistakes."

"Mistakes?" Lawrence frowned. "It looks good to me."

"Thank you." Sean set his cup down on the counter. "If you can't see them, I'm not going to point them out." He tilted his head slightly, looking at Lawrence from the corner of his eye. "You ever re-watch your old matches?"

"Sometimes."

"Are you ever satisfied with your performance at a match? Completely satisfied?"

Lawrence didn't have to think too hard about it. He'd been happy with the outcome more often than not, but he'd always made mistakes. Even his gold-winning bout hadn't been perfect. He'd just been lucky his small error hadn't cost him the match.

"It's rare," he admitted.

"Exactly." Sean set down his mug and crossed the open space to look up at the painting. "It's of my sister-in-law and my nephew," he said. "After she and my brother got divorced, neither of them wanted it. I guess she didn't because I'd painted it, and he didn't want a painting of his ex-wife hanging in his house." He shrugged, apparently not hurt by the rejection of his work. "But neither of them wanted to get rid of it, so they asked me if I would keep it for them."

"I like it," Lawrence said, hoping to ease any sting that Sean might have felt by being asked to take back his own work. "I'm not an artist, but I like how bright it is. It's, uh, cheerful I guess."

Sean beamed. Lawrence decided he liked this expression even more. "Thank you. That was what I was aiming for."

Unsure of what else he could say, Lawrence stuffed the rest of his croissant in his mouth.

"Whenever you're ready, you can sit down," Sean said. "Unless you'd prefer to stand? However you're more comfortable is fine."

It took a moment to swallow down the chunk of pastry. "I'll sit." The chair was pretty comfortable. Lawrence settled into it and let his gaze rest on Sean, enjoying the chance to stare at him.

Sean was wearing another t-shirt today. This one was red, slightly large on him, and had "Blood Donor" printed in white across the front. It was as paint-spattered as the one he'd worn the previous week.

"You're a blood donor?" Lawrence asked in surprise. He'd been barred from donating for his entire adult life by the draconian restrictions that still excluded gay men

"Donor...?" Sean blinked at him, then down at himself when Lawrence pointed at his shirt. Even then, it seemed to take him a moment. "Oh! No, I got this at a thrift store. I get all my painting clothes at thrift stores. I'm," his shoulders hunched uncomfortably, "I don't qualify to donate."

"Oh," Lawrence said awkwardly. "Me neither." He hunted for something else to talk about, but his tongue felt tied in knots.

Silence fell, awkward at first, but gradually settling into something easier, even cozy. Sean's shoulders relaxed as he began painting. There was no sound but the faint rumble of traffic.

Though he was short, no one would mistake Sean for a child, Lawrence thought. He had a sweet face, but it was beginning to show signs of being careworn, deepening wrinkles at the corners of his eyes and mouth, the occasional flash of silver in his brown curls. Lawrence wondered if he'd ever done a self-portrait. If Lawrence ever had the chance to make another trade with him, he would ask for one, he decided. He liked the idea of having a painting of Sean hanging in his apartment.

It was nice being here, existing together. A part of Lawrence was impatient to get up and move, any prolonged inaction being equal to laziness in his mind. But of course, he *was* doing something, he was modeling, and that required him to be still. He breathed in and out, deliberately deep and slow.

Sean's eyes darted to him and back to the canvas again and again as he worked, a bird with brown plumage and a red breast. Lawrence longed to have him perch on his wrist, to stroke his feathers.

He stopped himself from shaking his head against the ridiculous thoughts.

Sean kept working: glance, paint, glance, paint. The sun had shifted, Lawrence thought. How long had it been?

Sean was standing stock still, staring at the painting. His brush fell from his fingers, thumping down onto the rubber mat with a clunk.

"Sean?"

The art teacher's eyes were wide and his cheeks had lost all their color. He stared at the canvas for another long moment, blinking, then turned his gaze to Lawrence, who jumped to his feet. "Are you alright?"

"I'm—fine," Sean said. He didn't look fine. He seemed dazed, his eyes unfocused. He stole another glance at the painting.

"Did something go wrong?" Lawrence said, taking a step forward.

"No!" Sean shook his head, hurrying forward to meet Lawrence halfway. "It's fine! It's just—not finished. You can't look at it yet!"

"Okay. Okay, I won't." Lawrence wondered if Sean had made some sort of mistake. Maybe he'd ended up smearing or blotching the paint somehow and didn't want to admit it.

"Okay." Sean echoed. He gave his head a little shake and a strange laugh bubbled up in his throat. "I think, that is, I might need to lie down."

"Do you want to go to the doctor?" Lawrence said, alarmed. Had Sean had some sort of seizure that had made him smear his paint and drop his brush? Lawrence touched his forehead, but his skin felt normal.

Pulling his head back, Sean said, "No. No. I'm fine. Could you come back next week? Same time? If you can't it's okay."

"I'll come."

"Okay," Sean said again. "Good. That's good."

"Are you sure you're alright?"

"Fine!" Sean's voice was high and slightly strangled. "Truly, I'm fine. I just need to lie down for a few minutes."

"All right. Text me later. And if you need anything, a ride or anything, don't hesitate to call," Lawrence said as he reluctantly allowed himself to be herded to the door.

"I will. I will. I promise." Sean said. "I'll see you later."

The door closed between them.

~

They didn't see each other again until Tuesday. After kicking him out, Sean had texted Lawrence later in the day, apologizing and saying he'd remembered something important he had to do in the middle of painting. Lawrence was skeptical, but he was relieved that Sean had been clear-headed enough to text, and privately pleased that Sean had cared enough to do so.

Lawrence ended his own class even earlier than usual that Tuesday.

Sean's class was still painting when Lawrence stepped inside. The model was one of the younger ones this time, probably a student himself. The group stirred when Lawrence slipped in the door, and Sean glanced at the clock, then back at Lawrence. His eyebrows went up before descending into a puzzled frown. Lawrence just leaned against the back wall as he always did and waited.

The class was fidgety. No doubt they were used to Lawrence's entry being a signal that things would be wrapping up. His early entry threw them off. Lawrence felt a little bad for disrupting things.

"That's all for today," Sean said with a sigh. "Any questions about the assignment?" No raised hands, just the shuffling sounds of things being put away. "Any questions about anything else?"

Bobby spoke up, not even bothering with a raised hand. "About whether imbuing is miraculous or not," someone gave a snort and the kid's head whipped around for a moment before turning toward Sean again, "I wanted to ask whether you knew about the case where—"

"I'm afraid I don't have time to discuss imbuing today." Sean's voice was wintery quiet. Lawrence stared. He'd never once heard Sean turn down an opportunity to talk about imbuing. Was it because the kid had such an obnoxiously obvious agenda? Lawrence occasionally got students like that in his class, ones who had some kind of pet theory they wanted to push or proselytize about. He always shut them down.

The other students seemed equally stunned. "But—" the obnoxious student began.

"Are there any questions relevant to the classwork?" Sean asked. The students exchanged glances, but no one else spoke up.

"Very well. Class dismissed."

Lawrence waited until the students had filed out, the gaggle of them more subdued than usual. Once the room was quiet, he said, "You okay?"

"I'm fine," Sean said. He frowned over his supplies, not looking at Lawrence.

The dismissal was as clear as the one he'd given the students. Lawrence wanted to push, but he didn't quite dare. He stayed quiet as Sean finished clearing up, and they made their way down the familiar route to the other room in unusual silence. Just before they reached the door, Lawrence turned to Sean and said, "Hey, I won't push, but have I done anything wrong?"

Sean's eyes lost their distant look, narrowing in on him for the first time that afternoon. "Lawrence," he said, "It's not you. Something happened—that is, something came up, and it's made me distracted. I'm sorry."

"Don't apologize," Lawrence said. "I'm not trying to pry. But if there's something I can do, please let me know, won't you?" He hadn't expected that Sean's jaw would tighten at that.

"It's not really something you can help with," Sean said, his tone subdued. Somehow, it felt like a lie.

"Okay." Lawrence nodded and risked a hand on Sean's shoulder. "If anything changes, or if you think of anything, give me a call."

"I will." For a brief second, he lifted his hand and pressed his fingers against the back of Lawrence's. Then he let it fall and Lawrence pulled his own away, separating them.

"Will you still be able to join me for the concert this weekend?" Lawrence asked.

"Oh," Sean blinked, a guilty look flashing over his face. "That is this weekend, isn't it."

"If you can't, it's okay—"

"No, I want to go. I can make it."

"Okay," Lawrence said again.

"I'm sorry," Sean repeated. "It has nothing to do with you."

It still felt like a lie.

~

The day of the concert dawned bright and warm, but by the time evening fell, the temperature had turned cool and pleasant. They were due rain later, but it was supposed to hold off until that night.

Lawrence had cleaned his apartment within an inch of its life earlier that week, making good use of the time he normally would have spent drinking coffee with Sean since the art teacher called off their regular meetup. Lawrence wasn't a total slob or anything, but living alone, he didn't have much incentive to clean his bathrooms as often as he probably should have.

Sean looked good. He wore a button-down shirt, suit jacket and slacks, all surely tailored to fit him. Atop the ensemble he wore a long overcoat, which he slipped off and draped over his arm as he stepped inside.

"We'll want to leave in a few minutes," Lawrence said. "Can I get you anything before we go? Coffee? Tea? The coffee won't be as good as yours," he warned.

That brought a slight smile to Sean's lips. "I'm fine, thank you." They stood for a moment in awkward silence before Lawrence blurted, "Should we go, then?"

"Probably a good idea," Sean said. "Traffic gets bad this time of night."

Even with traffic, it didn't take them too long to arrive. Parking took a little longer, and it was a bit of a walk from the car to the theater, but the night air was crisp and exhilarating in Lawrence's lungs as they strolled through the public park that abutted the theater. The green space was filled with well-lit, winding paths. Lawrence savored the fresh air and the smell of greenery, and wondered if he could get away with taking Sean's arm. Last week he might have gone for it, but Sean's sudden distance held him at bay, uncertain of his welcome.

Had it been a mistake to invite Sean on a date? He *had* spoken of wanting to attend the concert. Lawrence just hoped the art teacher wouldn't be too distracted to enjoy it.

The theater was old, with small, cramped seats not designed for modern bodies. Sean settled into his and looked up at Lawrence with the first genuine full smile Lawrence had seen from him in a week.

"No stadium seating," Sean said. "Normally I wouldn't be able to see over the person in front of me, but since these are such good seats, it's not an issue." They weren't in the very front row, but they were in the front row of their section, with an aisle and a drop down to the next row.

A swell of pride and pleasure expanded in Lawrence's chest. Sean's height hadn't been one of his considerations when choosing the seats—something he now realized had been an oversight—but he'd managed to get ones with a good view anyway.

"Is it frequently a problem for you?" Lawrence asked.

"Most newer places have stadium seating these days," Sean said, "though I've run into exceptions. I went to one outdoor venue where it turned out that the lower seats closer to the stage had tiered but not stadium spacing." He grinned ruefully. "I was in the second row. This guy sat down in front of me, he must have been six and a half feet tall. I spent the entire concert craning my neck and trying to see around him."

Frowning, Lawrence said, "Couldn't you have asked him to switch with you?" He wondered uncomfortably if there had ever been short people stuck behind him when he hadn't realized it. He wasn't that tall, only just under six feet, but he was tall enough to block the view of plenty of people.

"I could have, but then the people behind me wouldn't have been able to see. He was *really* tall. Besides, he'd paid for a front row seat. It was a good life lesson for me. I learned to check the venue more carefully before buying tickets." Sighing, he pressed his shoulders against the plush seatback. "That was a long time ago, though. These days, I usually choose venues where I can stay standing. People will almost always let me go in front of them, since they can see over my head anyway," he said, his grin turning conspiratorial.

Should Lawrence have tried to get standing tickets for their date?

He was fairly sure this theater didn't have a standing area, but he hadn't looked beyond the expensive orchestra seats. Well, beyond asking his publicist to get him the best seats she could. Thank goodness she'd gotten them ones that worked. He'd have to give her a bonus.

"For concerts like this it doesn't matter quite as much, since mostly we'll be listening, not watching. Still, it's nice to be able to see." Sean turned his gaze to the stage, where the orchestra was beginning to file in. "They'll be starting soon."

The first half of the concert went quickly. Lawrence wasn't all that interested in the music, but he couldn't help stealing glances at Sean. Sean seemed happy, a slight smile on his lips, his gaze focused on the players or the conductor, his eyes occasionally closed during a particularly poignant part. Lawrence itched to reach for his hand, but he didn't want to distract his companion from his enjoyment.

At the intermission, Lawrence rose. "Do you want to stretch your legs?"

"I'm good," Sean said. His neck was tilted at what looked like an uncomfortable angle, an odd tension sitting in his shoulders.

"Do you want anything? I can bring you some water or something."

Shaking his head, Sean said, "No thank you."

"All right. I'll be right back." Lawrence rose and headed over to the bathroom. He didn't envy the people standing outside the women's bathroom in a long line. At least it seemed to be moving. After he'd taken care of business, he hurried back to his seat, waving his hands to dry them.

There was a crease between Sean's brows, but his expression lightened as Lawrence settled beside him into the too-tight seat. "Are you enjoying the show?" Sean asked.

He was, though probably not for the same reasons that Sean was. "Yes. Are you?"

"Very much so. It was kind of you to ask me. Thank you."

It hadn't been *kindness* that motivated Lawrence, but he wasn't sure how to correct Sean without sounding like a creep. "You're welcome." He hunted for something to say. "The imbued piece isn't until the end."

"Yes," Sean said. "Imbued music only carries the imbued properties when it's heard live. I'm looking forward to it."

"Have you heard any imbued music before?" Lawrence asked.

"Twice. It was unforgettable. I've been very lucky to have so many opportunities."

"Why aren't they performed more often? Are they difficult?"

"Not exactly. Imbued music is often surprisingly simple on the page," Sean said, leaning a little toward Lawrence as he explained. "But it's difficult to perform perfectly. It must be performed precisely as intended or it won't carry the imbued qualities. Even the best musicians don't always get it right."

"So we might *not* get an imbued performance today?" Lawrence straightened.

"That's always a risk. I'm sure it was in the fine print when you bought the tickets," Sean said. "But the violinist is a genius, so I wouldn't worry too much."

Lawrence fumed silently. He hadn't paid all that money to risk not getting an imbued performance for Sean!

"It will be fine," Sean said soothingly. "Even if we don't get to see the imbued piece, the concert's been lovely so far. I'm so glad you asked me."

"Oh." The heat of anger melted into something else, a warmth that Lawrence could feel crawling into his cheeks. "Me too," he mumbled.

"It's a sad fact that the people who are talented enough to perform imbued pieces often say that they don't enjoy doing so."

"What? Why not?"

"For an imbued piece to be performed perfectly, the musician can't bring anything of themselves into the performance. There's no freedom to interpret the piece, no changing the tempo or adding anything or leaving anything out. There are some performers who like that, who say that all music should be performed as close to 'as written' as possible. But many of the most well-known performers became famous for the emotion they bring to their performances."

"So you have to be like a machine to play an imbued piece?" Lawrence asked.

"Not...exactly. You still have to be human. You have to be as affected by the piece as anyone listening to it. But you can't put your own stamp on it. Performers have talked about how it's like being a 'vessel' or a 'channel' for the imbued piece. The piece must flow through them without being affected by them."

"Huh." Lawrence picked up the program that had slipped to the floor when he'd risen. It still sounded a bit like mystical mumbo-jumbo to him, but most things that had to do with imbuing did. He searched for another question he could ask, but the lights began to dim, signaling that the second half of the concert was beginning.

~

The second half of the concert was much like the first. Sean watched the performers and listened raptly. Lawrence watched Sean as much as he dared.

It wasn't until the very end that they brought out the violinist. The lights on the orchestra went dark, with only a single spotlight on the petite woman. According to the program, she'd been born in China and had begun developing her musical skill from a young age, quickly proving to be a prodigy. Her dress was simple and black, cut to allow free movement of her arms and shoulders. After making her way to the center of the stage, she bowed, lifted the violin, and closed her eyes.

The first few notes hung in the air, shivering and crystalline. As she played, sorrow sank into Lawrence's chest, a heavy grief that pulled and weighed. He barely noticed the burning in his eyes, the sob that rose and caught in his throat. The lights blurred, the violinist becoming indistinct.

Something shifted. The lament took on a new note, a sweet underlying feeling that began to grow, piercing through the anguish like the first flower after a long winter. Little by little the new feeling swelled, the sadness transforming into a slow, gentle hope, which in turn transmuted into joy.

The weight lifted. As it lightened, Lawrence felt as though he would float up out of his seat, carried by sheer elation. The violinist was blurrier than ever.

The piece drew to an end with a wave of solemn exultation.

Lawrence became aware of the tears streaming down his face, the way he was gasping for breath. He lifted a hand to wipe his eyes and found it caught, a tissue pressed into it. Looking to his benefactor, he met Sean's gaze.

Sean's eyes were red, his face wet with tears as well. He smiled at Lawrence, and Lawrence found himself smiling back, his heart still pounding, the flood of wonder only just beginning to recede.

Someone started to clap. Lawrence hastily wiped his eyes and nose before shoving the tissue in his pocket and clapping harder than he had all night. The conductor came on stage and handed the violinist a white handkerchief. She accepted and wiped her own eyes before bowing.

The applause was thunderous.

"There won't be an encore," Sean said, leaning over to Lawrence and raising his voice to be heard above the din. "What could possibly follow that?"

~

The date had been a success, Lawrence thought as the audience began to file out around them. He couldn't feel embarrassed about weeping during the imbued song—not when everyone else in the audience had, too. It would have been impossible *not* to.

Sean still hadn't risen. He shifted slightly in his narrow seat, his eyebrows drawing into a frown.

"Ready to go?" Lawrence said. "Or did you want to stay a bit longer?"

Shifting again, Sean opened his mouth. Pain flickered across his face, there and gone lightning fast.

"Are you okay?" Lawrence stood up and held out his hand. "Got a cramp?" Sean hadn't gotten up during intermission. "These old seats are terrible on the back."

"Yes," Sean said through gritted teeth. "I…" he swallowed and closed his eyes for a moment. Lawrence felt a stab of worry.

"What's wrong?"

"I'm," Sean shifted forward, then froze, his breath catching in what was so obviously pain that Lawrence found himself surging

151

forward to try to help somehow.

"What do you need?"

Shaking his head, Sean said, "It's—it's chronic. When I sit for too long, my back," he grimaced, not looking at Lawrence. "I took some painkillers before you picked me up, but," his lips twisted unhappily.

Guilt roiled in Lawrence's stomach. He shouldn't have invited Sean. He should have gotten different tickets. "What can I do?"

"Nothing." Sean braced himself on the arms and began to lever himself upright, only to collapse back with a small, hurt sound.

"Do you want me to—to carry you?" Lawrence offered. He was confident that he could carry Sean a short distance, at least, though probably not all the way back to the car.

"No!" Sean glared at him. "I'm not a *child.*"

"Of course. I'm sorry." Lawrence lifted his hands placatingly. Sean rubbed a hand over his face.

"No, I'm sorry. I shouldn't have yelled. If worse comes to worst we can see if they have a wheelchair. But if I can just get up, we won't need it. It will be slow, but I can walk."

"Can you brace against me?" Lawrence offered. The theater was emptying quickly.

"I can try." Lawrence offered his arm, and Sean gripped it. With the air of one ripping off a band aid, he pushed himself to his feet. His face was pale, his forehead covered with sweat. "I'm so sorry about this."

"Not your fault," Lawrence said, and meant it.

"It is, actually. I shouldn't have accepted your invitation," Sean sighed. "I knew this would probably happen. I just—I really wanted to…" he looked away, his lips pressed together.

"You wanted to see the imbued performance," Lawrence finished for him. Sean glanced at him, opened his mouth as though to respond, then closed it again. "I'm sorry, I would have gotten standing tickets if I'd known."

"Don't *apologize.*" Sean muttered under his breath and, clinging to Lawrence's arm, took a small step forward, then another. He was still bent over, but gradually managed to straighten out.

Slowly, they worked their way up the aisle. There was no one to block their progress, the rest of the audience having long since made its way out. It was a bit like being in a deserted classroom, echoing and strange. Janitors arrived and began cleaning the aisles and stage. They ignored Lawrence and Sean, for which Lawrence was grateful.

It took them fifteen minutes to make it to the front of the theater and up to the door.

It was raining. Not just a romantic sprinkle, either, but a hard downpour. Lawrence squinted out at it and made a decision. "Stay here," he said. "I'll get the car and pick you up."

"I can just get a taxi or an Uber," Sean said. "You don't have to—"

"I have to pick up my car no matter what," Lawrence insisted. "Just wait here, okay? I'll be back as soon as I can." Sean still wouldn't meet his eyes, but he gave a nod.

"Thank you. I'm so sorry."

"The rain is definitely not your fault," Lawrence said, "and there's no need for both of us to get wet." He gave Sean a nod in turn and started sprinting.

He was soaked to the skin by the time he got to his car. Sliding into the front seat, he slammed the door, shoved the key in the ignition, cranked up the heater, and drove as quickly as he could to where Sean stood in front of the theater, just under the eaves. The rain made a curtain in front of him until he was as blurred as the violinist had been. Lawrence pulled up to the curb directly in front of him and leaned across to swing open the door. Sean was standing a little straighter now, and to Lawrence's relief, managed to cross the small space and fold himself into the car fairly quickly.

"I'll get you home as soon as I can," said Lawrence. Sean reached down and leaned the seat back as far as it would go, until he was nearly prone.

"Thank you," he said softly. He sounded miserable. Defeated.

Lawrence wished he had any idea what to say. Instead, he just drove as quickly as he dared through the pouring rain.

~

There was a substitute teaching the art class when Lawrence arrived early the following Tuesday. Sean had texted to cancel their portrait sitting that had been scheduled the day after their date. Lawrence had told himself not to worry about it, Sean was probably just tired after — after all that.

His absence from the classroom was more concerning. Their date had been on Friday and it was already Tuesday. Lawrence asked the substitute if she knew why he hadn't come, but she just shrugged and said, "They don't tell me anything." One of the students who was taking another one of Sean's classes confirmed that Sean had been gone on Monday as well.

Later that afternoon Lawrence headed to the campus coffee shop alone and dithered about whether he should text Sean or not. What if Sean was sleeping and Lawrence woke him up? What if he didn't want to hear from Lawrence after things had gone so disastrously at the end of their date? Was he just sick? Was he still in pain?

Then again, maybe Sean needed help. Maybe he would appreciate it if Lawrence reached out.

Finally, Lawrence typed, 'Missed you today. I hope you feel better soon' and hit 'Send' before he could change his mind.

He stayed at the coffee shop until late, but Sean never responded.

~

On Thursday, Sean was back in his classroom. He looked tired and thinner to Lawrence's eyes. Haggard.

His class seemed more subdued than usual, too. Sean glanced at Lawrence when he came in, then ignored him, not meeting his eyes. Sean didn't even ask if there were questions at the end of the class, just dismissed the students a few minutes early and waited through the usual shuffling and chatting.

The model, definitely a student this time, was fully dressed by the time the room was half empty. He hiked up his jeans, which looked to be a size too big for him, and headed for the front of the room. "Um," he said, and glanced at Lawrence surreptitiously.

It took a visible moment for the student's presence to register to Sean. Then, "Oh, of course," Sean said. "Sorry, Sam, I'm scatterbrained today."

"It's totally fine. I really appreciate this opportunity," Sam said. Sean went over to his desk and unlocked one of the drawers. Taking out some cash, he handed it to the student, who shot another guilty glance at Lawrence before taking it. "Thank you again."

"It's no problem," Sean said. "Let me know if you can't make rent again, all right? I'll see if I can get you on the schedule."

The poor kid flushed. "Yeah, okay." Ducking his head and avoiding Lawrence's eyes, he hurried out of the room.

Lawrence felt a fond smile pulling at his lips. If the kid were on the normal modeling schedule, he'd have received a check from the school, not cash from Sean. "Paying the models out of your own pocket?"

Meeting his gaze at last, Sean responded with a rueful shrug. "Not all of them. But the school has a lot of rules about who can be a model and how they can be paid. Generally they don't allow students to be models."

"No?" Lawrence recalled a fair number of times he'd seen a young person doing the modeling and assumed they were a student.

"No." Sean's face darkened. "Sam's financial aid check was delayed. Some kind of snafu in the accounting office or something. He came to me and told me he was going to have to drop out. So," he gave an awkward laugh, "I offered him a job."

Pushing off the back wall, Lawrence strolled to the front of the room. It smelled of paint, familiar and pleasant. "I once arranged for a 'private scholarship' for a kid who couldn't afford his own fencing equipment," he offered.

"Oh," Sean's expression lightened again, "that's a good idea. I'll have to remember that one."

"It ended up being more of a pain than I thought it would," Lawrence admitted. "The Financial Aid office asked me all kinds of questions about what the scholarship was and what corporation or family was sponsoring it. If you want to do something like that, let me know. I finally found someone who helped me arrange it behind the scenes without too much fuss."

"I'll do that." Sean sighed. "It's a terrible temptation. I wish I could help all of them."

"I know." Warmth collected in Lawrence's chest. He wanted to reach out to Sean, to touch him. Instead he shoved his hands into his jacket pockets. "Hey," he said, "how are you doing?"

Stiffening, Sean said, "I'm all right."

"I'm sorry about Friday."

"You have nothing to apologize for," Sean said bitterly. "I shouldn't have accepted in the first place. I *knew* my back wouldn't be able to take it. I just," he stopped and sighed again, running a hand through his curls.

"Did you—did you at least enjoy the concert itself?" Lawrence couldn't help asking. "Were you in pain the whole time?" It hadn't seemed like it, but maybe Sean had been hiding it.

"No! No, the concert was wonderful. I was fine until I tried to stand up."

Relief washed through Lawrence. He felt his shoulders unwind slightly. "I'm glad you got to have that much, at least."

Frowning, Sean turned away and started to fiddle with things on his desk. "Look," he said, "I don't know why you asked someone like me in the first place—"

"Someone 'like you'?"

Waving a hand down his body in a sharp gesture, Sean said, "There's not much about me that's desirable." His face twisted with ugly humor. "There's not much to me, period. Add to that the fact that I can't even sit down at a restaurant, or take a long plane ride, or—"

"I don't care about any of that!" Lawrence's outburst made Sean's head snap up. "I—you—" He gritted his teeth, struggling to put into words his attraction and affection. "I like you," he said at last, and felt himself grow hot with embarrassment at how immature he sounded. "I like being with you," he tried again. "I like listening to you talk about art, about imbuing, about your students. I like telling you about my fencing matches. I like spending time with you. You're clever and funny and kind. And the fact that you're short doesn't bother me." If anything, Lawrence admitted to himself, he kind of liked it.

Sean's eyes were wide and stunned. "But," he said, giving his head a little shake, "You—you're *you*. You're a gold medalist, you're handsome and rich and could have anyone you wanted!"

"Including you?"

Sean reared back at the quick response. The flush in his cheeks darkened. "I—" He stopped. His throat moved in a swallow. "I mean, of *course*—"

Stepping forward, Lawrence took his hands. "Can we try again? Go on another date? There's going to be an exhibition of imbued items next month—"

A disbelieving laugh stopped him. "You really—after that disastrous date, even after I could barely walk to the front of the theater, after you had to run in the rain to get the car—you still want to?"

"Yeah, I do. And I would have had to run in the rain anyway," Lawrence said. "I wouldn't have let a date go out in that, whether he had back problems or not."

"Well," Sean gave him a shaky smile, "I mean, if you're certain."

"I'm certain." Lawrence squeezed Sean's delicate, paint-stained hands. Sean stared up at him, still uncertain, but with hope creeping into his eyes.

"All right."

~

"Welcome." Lawrence handed Sean a paper bag and stepped over the threshold. Sean sniffed rapturously. "Ooh, croissants again?"

"Danishes," Lawrence said.

Sean peered into the bag like a curious robin. "They smell amazing. Coffee?"

"Please." The front room was filled with sunshine. "I'm glad it didn't rain," he said, slipping off his shoes and heading over to the wall of windows that looked out over the city.

"Was that a possibility?" Sean said from the kitchen area.

"There was a chance of it. I figured you probably wouldn't want me to sit for you if it was cloudy."

"Astute of you," Sean said. He came to stand next to Lawrence and offered him a mug, the same one that Lawrence had used last time. Lawrence took a sip and closed his eyes.

"That's good coffee."

Chuckling, Sean said, "Is it the coffee that's good or the caffeine?"

"Why not both?"

With a snort, Sean headed back to the kitchen and pulled out two small plates. "What kind do you want? It looks like there's apple, cream cheese, and blueberry."

"Blueberry, please," Lawrence said, "Unless you want that one."

"No, I'll take cream cheese." Lawrence stretched and yawned, then turned to catch Sean watching him. Lawrence smirked and Sean dropped his eyes and took a sip. "I wanted to try a different pose today," he said.

"A different pose? Are you going to re-do the painting?"

"Yes. The other one," Sean tore off a piece from the edge of his pastry, "won't work."

"What happened to it?"

"Sometimes an art piece just doesn't come together," Sean said, his voice curiously flat. "Even professionals have bad days. But I have an idea for something that I think will look really good if you're willing."

"What is it?"

Stuffing the bit of pastry in his mouth, Sean rinsed his fingers and mumbled, "Be right back." He disappeared into what must be his bedroom. Lawrence caught a glimpse of a small room barely big enough to fit what looked like a Queen-sized bed before the door closed behind him. Half a minute later the door swung open again and Sean stepped through. He was carrying an épée.

No, not an épée, Lawrence realized as Sean brought it over, a *rapier*. It was either vintage or a very good reproduction. Sean offered it to him, flat across his hands, and Lawrence put down his coffee and picked it up.

It felt different from the ones he was used to, not an electric competition épée but a deadly weapon. "Where did you get this?"

"It belonged to my grandfather," Sean said. "He collected all kinds of things. This has a case and everything. It's authentic."

Nodding, Lawrence examined it more closely. "It's sharp," he noted.

"That was how my grandfather kept it," Sean said. "Seeing it for the first time is what made me want to study fencing years ago. I didn't get very far. My back problems started getting worse around then and left me incapacitated for long stretches of time. But grandpa knew I'd always liked the piece and left it to me in his will."

"I'm sorry," Lawrence said. For Sean's inability to pursue fencing? For the loss of his grandfather? Lawrence wasn't sure.

Sean merely nodded his acceptance, so it didn't matter. "If you're willing, I thought I might paint you wielding it?"

"Of course," Lawrence said. "I would be honored." He squinted at the sky. Sun was streaming through the window, but in the distance he could see the billowing thunderhead of another late-spring storm. "Though we won't have the light for long at this rate," he said.

"All the more reason to get started," Sean said cheerfully. Their relationship had gone back to the way it had been before the concert, friendly and warm, but no more. Lawrence was hopeful, though. They'd scheduled a second date, this one an exhibition where they could walk around and look at the items rather than sitting in one place. Lawrence had been keeping an eye out for other opportunities as well: restaurants where one could stand weren't as uncommon as he'd feared. And while their interactions were back to normal, every once in a while he'd catch Sean looking at him, sometimes with bewilderment, a few times with a heat in his eyes that made the breath stop in Lawrence's throat.

They worked out a pose for him: one interesting enough to satisfy Sean but which Lawrence could maintain for an extended period of time.

Sean began to paint as Lawrence sank into his breathing, holding still and steady.

The shift in light happened abruptly. One moment it was golden; the next it was a rapidly-dimming grey. Sean made an annoyed sound. "Damn. It looks like that storm's arrived. I'd hoped to have a few more minutes. Ah well."

Lawrence carefully set down the rapier and stretched, shaking out stiff muscles. "I can come back next week," he said hopefully. Sean fumbled with his brush, clattering it against the palette.

"You must have better things to do," he said, his eyes down.

"No," Lawrence said. "I like spending time with you."

An appealing flush darkened Sean's cheeks. "How can you just say things like that?" he complained. "Out of nowhere, with no warning whatsoever?"

Shrugging, Lawrence said, "It's the truth."

Giving a little huff, Sean said, "I'll be right back," and disappeared into the bathroom, taking the brush with him.

Lawrence could feel himself smiling. The sky was heavy and dark with clouds, but the rain hadn't started yet. Maybe Sean would invite him to stay and wait out the storm? Lawrence lost himself in a happy little fantasy of how they might occupy their time before making himself focus on the now. He picked up the rapier and tried some moves with it, feeling its weight and analyzing the ways it differed from the competition épées he was familiar with.

Even afterward, Lawrence could never quite say how it had happened. He'd gone through a couple of sequences of movements, parrying and thrusting, when a flash of lightning split the sky. He flinched, his attention drawn away for a crucial second.

The blade encountered resistance.

It was Sean.

The blade sank into his chest.

Horror flashed through Lawrence. Instinctively he yanked the sword out of the wound, immediately realizing that he shouldn't have done so. But it was too late. Sean gave a gasp and crumpled to his knees, hands flying to his chest.

Thunder cracked like the report of a gun.

"No!" Lawrence surged forward, one hand going helplessly, uselessly, to the bleeding wound.

That had been a heart hit.

"Sean!"

An ambulance. Lawrence needed to call an ambulance. Maybe they could — maybe he could still —

He couldn't make himself move. He'd *felt* the rapier penetrate. He'd seen the look on Sean's face. Sean was dead. He was dead.

Pure grief washed over Lawrence in a wave, swamping him. Drowning him.

Gone.

Sean would be gone.

The chest under Lawrence's hand rose and fell. Sean was breathing. He was still breathing. People had survived worse. Not even daring to hope, Lawrence moved to lay Sean down. He would call for help. He would —

A hand wrapped around his. It was slick, sticky with blood.

"Wait." Sean was shaking.

"I need to call an ambulance!" Lawrence's voice came out in a choked whisper. *He* was the one shaking, he realized. He felt sick and cold, a heavy weight in his stomach. He tried to pull away, but Sean's slippery grip tightened.

"Lawrence, wait." Sean's voice was remarkably steady. He lifted his other hand and tugged awkwardly at his t-shirt. "It's — I think it's all right."

"What?" How could he possibly be all right? Lawrence had just seen a couple of inches of sharpened steel sink into his chest, directly over his heart. Was Sean in shock?

"Look. Lawrence, *look*." All Lawrence could see was blood. Sean pulled his hand against his chest. "It's gone."

"What?" Lawrence said again. He tried to pull away, but Sean pressed harder against his skin.

His unbroken skin.

Lightning flashed, blinding.

"How?"

Thunder rolled and crashed.

"I felt it." Sean looked up at him, eyes wide and wet. "When you touched me. I felt it."

"Felt what?" The rapier slicing into him? Of course he'd felt it!

"You healed me. Lawrence, you imbued me. Like the curse, but in reverse."

Lawrence's hand slid in the blood that was very definitely still there, skidding over the place where it should have still been spilling out. It was whole, without even a scar. Opening his mouth to speak, Lawrence choked on a sob instead. "You're okay."

"Yes. I'm okay. I'm alive."

"I killed you. I almost killed you."

"It was an accident," Sean said gently. "And you fixed it."

"You're okay," Lawrence said again, "you're okay." He couldn't seem to say anything else.

"Yes." Sean wrapped his arms around him, pulling him close. "I'm alright. Everything's alright."

The skies opened, rain pouring down like a faucet.

~

The flood of overwhelming panic and all-encompassing relief in quick succession left Lawrence jittery and exhausted, worn to a raveling. Sean was surprisingly composed once the initial shock wore off. He held Lawrence through the storm, through the shudders and strangled sobs. Afterward he gave him tea and a damp washcloth to wipe his face once Lawrence had calmed enough to use them.

"Thanks." Lawrence pressed the washcloth against his eyes for a long moment, then accepted a tissue from Sean to blow his nose. "Fuck. I can't believe it. *Fuck.*" Normally Lawrence didn't swear at all—it was a bad habit to get into, both as a teacher and as a gold medalist whose words tended to be recorded and remembered. If there was ever an occasion for it, this was it.

A warm hand settled on his back, rubbing up and down. Lawrence looked over at Sean and tried to smile, though it still felt uncomfortably tremulous.

"Want to split the last danish?"

"Sure." The word was innocuous, automatic, meaningless. The hand on his back kept stroking up and down, slow and easy. He closed his eyes and leaned back against the touch.

"I'll get it." Sean rose smoothly, then froze. Lawrence looked up at him. Sean's face was twisted in a puzzled frown.

"You okay?" Lawrence asked.

Blinking, Sean gave a nod. "I'm fine," he said. He went to the kitchen area and Lawrence turned to watch him as he took the danish out of the fridge. "Why do you always bring three pastries?" Sean called back to him.

It took a moment for Lawrence's sluggish mind to parse the question. "The—the bakery has a special every Saturday, buy two and get one free."

"Ah."

Sean fiddled with the coffee machine. A knife clinked against a plate as he cut the danish in half. Soon he was back, kneeling down beside where Lawrence still sat on the wooden floor. There was a reddish-brown stain on the floor. On his sweater, too, he realized vaguely as he looked down at himself. Sean set the plate next to him.

Reaching over, Lawrence grabbed his hands. "Can I kiss you?" His voice was harsh and thin. He hadn't even known he was going to ask until the words were hanging in the air between them. His heart dropped momentarily when Sean tugged his hands out of Lawrence's grip, but then he lifted them to Lawrence's face. Those delicate fingers rested lightly on his cheeks, forgiving, gentle, warm. Leaning forward, Sean pressed his lips to Lawrence's.

It was a fleeting thing, a quick touch of warmth. Lawrence leaned forward in turn, chasing the sensation, wanting more. He deepened the kiss, a little at a time.

Sean smiled against his mouth and let Lawrence in.

~

Opening his eyes, Lawrence blinked at the ceiling. It wasn't his ceiling. He stared at it, his mind still floating and disconnected, before a shift in the bed beside him drew his attention.

Sean was curled up next to him.

The previous night returned in a rush, making his heart speed and his body tense. Without moving, he let his eyes roam over as much of Sean as he could see. It wasn't much; Sean had burrowed under the sheet, only his nose and the top of his head sticking out.

He was breathing, the mound under the sheet rising and falling in a gentle, even rhythm.

The room was small, the bed taking up most of it. Lawrence wondered why Sean had a Queen-sized. He could have fit into a Full easily, or even a Twin.

Directly opposite the bed a TV stood atop a dresser. The wall to the right was mostly window, grey with morning light. The left-hand wall had canvases leaning against it, most of them finished paintings, next to the door that led back into the apartment.

Sean stirred, drawing his attention again. As Lawrence watched, Sean's eyes fluttered open. Finding Lawrence's gaze on him, he startled, then smiled.

"Good morning," Lawrence said.

"Good morning," Sean replied. His voice was slightly hoarse. "How are you feeling?"

"I should be asking you that."

"I'm fine." He tugged the sheet down and gestured to his pajama-covered chest. "Still in one piece."

Some of the tension bled out of Lawrence's shoulders. "Good."

"Thanks to you," Sean added.

Lawrence shrugged. "You got hurt because of me. I'm just relieved you're okay." He drew a breath. It shook a little. "We got lucky."

Reaching across the space between them, Sean said, "It was an accident." Lawrence took his hand.

"Accident or not, you would have been just as dead if—" the words stuck in his throat.

Sean squeezed his hand. "I'm fine. Truly." He stroked a thumb over the back of Lawrence's fingers, letting the silence lengthen until Lawrence had gotten ahold of himself. "Do you want some breakfast? I've got eggs."

"Sure."

With a nod, Sean gave his hand another squeeze, then rolled over and got out of bed. Rather than sitting up, he slid his legs out and to the floor, then levered himself up with his hands. Straightening, he turned back to look at Lawrence. He was wearing an odd expression, his eyes unfocused, his brows drawn together and his lips slightly parted.

"Sean?"

Blinking, Sean gave himself a little shake. "I'm fine. Just..." his brows drew together more tightly, then his expression cleared. "It's nothing."

"You sure?"

"Yes. Everything's fine. More than fine." His smile returned as he met Lawrence's eyes.

Lawrence smiled back and sat up in turn, tugging at his borrowed shirt. After making out for a while the previous night, they'd taken turns showering. None of Sean's regular clothes fit Lawrence, but he'd dug up an old t-shirt he'd gotten as a freebie that was only a little tight, so Lawrence had worn that and his own underwear to bed, curling up and falling asleep with his hand resting lightly on Sean's heart.

He pulled on his pants, which had fortunately missed the worst of the blood, and followed Sean into the front room that served as living room, kitchen, and studio.

~

They made breakfast without talking about what had happened, easily moving around each other in the kitchen and eating while leaning back against the counter, side by side.

When they'd finished, Sean washed and Lawrence dried, setting the dishes back in their places on the lowest shelf of the cabinets.

When they'd finished, Sean poured them each a second cup of coffee, emptying the pot. Taking his mug, a nice one with a rainbow on it, he strolled over and looked out the big window. The sun had risen while they were eating, and the light streaming in had a bright, clear quality.

"Where'd you get that mug?" Lawrence asked, following him.

"It was a gift at the last Pride." He held it up. "It's pretty, isn't it?"

"Yeah."

"Do you want to tell people?" Sean said.

It took Lawrence a moment to realize what he meant. "About the imbuing? I don't know."

"You're already famous, being a gold medalist. This would probably increase your fame, make you recognizable to even more people." He turned and cocked his head a little. "That could be a good thing or a bad thing."

"Yeah." Lawrence shook himself and rolled his shoulders. "Let me think about it."

Sean nodded and finished his coffee. He set down his mug with a sharp clank on the counter and straightened. "I have something to show you."

Lawrence looked at him curiously.

"Wait here?" Sean asked. He fidgeted, not quite meeting Lawrence's eyes. Whatever it was he wanted to show Lawrence, it was making him nervous.

"Of course." Lawrence kept his back to the room, gazing out at the awakening city as he finished his coffee. He could hear the other man padding and shuffling behind him, then the sound of the bedroom door opening and closing.

The smell of blood lingered. Lawrence hoped it wouldn't be too hard to remove from the floor. He'd have to look up the best way to do it. The window was big, but had no visible sash. "Does the window open?" he called.

"Unfortunately not," Sean called back. The bedroom door opened again and he continued in a more normal tone, "I think they were afraid that people would jump out of them. Which is silly, anyone with any sense would just go up to the roof if they wanted to do something like that."

"You can go out on the roof?"

"Well, technically one isn't supposed to, but the door was already jimmied long before I moved in. It's not the prettiest spot—a couple of smokers like to go up there and leave their butts all over the place—but the view makes up for it."

"I'd like to see it."

"Maybe we can go up there later."

"Sure."

The sound of a breath being drawn. "This is it."

Lawrence turned. The easel Sean had been using had been set to face him instead. There was a cloth hanging over it. Sean took hold of a corner of the cloth and tugged until it slid off, revealing Lawrence's face.

"This is the—" *portrait?* he'd meant to say, but the word died on his tongue. The version of him in the painting was in three-quarter view, gazing at some distant point. As Lawrence watched, his copy turned and looked directly at him, his dark eyes intense.

Sucking in a breath, Lawrence put a hand on his chest as a surge of longing rushed through him. It was a little disconcerting to feel while staring at his own face, but then, it wasn't his emotion. It was Sean's.

Sean had imbued his portrait.

"This is," Lawrence said, the words still sticking in his throat, "this is why you started over."

"Yes." The man in the portrait turned aside again, the cycle beginning anew. Lawrence pulled his eyes away and looked at Sean instead.

"You weren't going to show it to me?"

Shaking his head, Sean slumped a little. "How could I?"

"How could you *not?*" Would Sean really have kept this from him? From everyone?

"I didn't want you to feel pressured," Sean whispered. "To make you feel like you *had* to — to reciprocate."

"And if I wanted to reciprocate? If I did — if I *do* reciprocate?"

Flushing, Sean said, "I would have told you eventually."

"When? On our wedding night?" Lawrence said, then froze. "I mean, if we got married. Someday."

Sean gave a hiccupping little laugh. "I know what you meant." He looked at the painting, then looked away. "It's just, it's so personal."

That was fair enough. Lawrence looked at the painting again, watched it meet his eyes, felt the same rush of longing. If that was how Sean felt about him, Lawrence could understand not wanting to share it with the world, or even with Lawrence himself.

But he had. "Why now?" Lawrence said.

Staring at him disbelievingly, Sean said, "You *imbued* me. You saved my life. You kissed me." He flung his hands up. "I think it's 'eventually'!"

Laughter bubbled up in Lawrence's throat. He shook his head and didn't even try to hold it back. Sean scowled, but couldn't maintain it in the face of Lawrence's mirth. His lips started twitching until, in spite of himself, he broke as well.

They laughed until they were breathless, until tears came to their eyes, until their faces hurt from it. Every time one of them would start to calm down, the other would start giggling again.

Eventually they did manage to calm down. Lawrence wiped his streaming eyes and accepted a glass of water, draining half of it in one gulp before setting it on the kitchen counter. "All right," he said. Reaching out, he wound an arm around Sean's waist. "It's 'eventually'. What now?"

Sighing, Sean set down his own water and leaned against Lawrence's chest. He felt good in Lawrence's arms, warm and precious and right. Closing his eyes, Lawrence brought his other hand up to stroke through Sean's curls and lightly cup the back of his head.

"I don't know," Sean said, his voice low. "We — we probably should still date and — and all that. Right? Just because we, that is…"

he trailed off.

"Whatever you want," Lawrence said. "We can keep spending time together at work, with motion studies and coffee dates."

"Oh." Sean lifted his head. "Were those dates?"

"I was never quite certain myself, to be honest," Lawrence admitted.

Sean's lips twitched. He buried his face against Lawrence's chest again. "I don't know," he said again. "We've known each other a long time. But this is new. I'm afraid to rush things."

"Nothing has to change," Lawrence said. We'll see each other like we always have. And maybe get together outside of work sometimes. Go to an exhibition. I can model for you, or you can come to one of my matches. I'm sure I can arrange a place where you can stand and watch them, if you like."

"I very much *would* like." Sean lifted his head once more, and took a reluctant step back, trailing his hand around Lawrence's torso and to the center of his chest before letting it fall as they separated. Something flickered over his face, his lips parting as though he wanted to say something else, then pressing together again.

"What is it?" Lawrence said.

"Nothing," Sean said. He picked up his water and finished it before glancing at the window. "Do you want to go up to the roof?"

"Sure."

It was up a couple of flights of stairs. Lawrence hoped it wasn't putting a strain on Sean's back, but he figured Sean knew his own limits best.

In fact, Sean seemed more energetic than Lawrence had ever seen him. He easily kept up with Lawrence, despite his shorter legs. When they reached the top, Lawrence stopped, staring at a large, "WARNING: ALARM WILL SOUND" sign on the door.

"Like I said, someone jimmied it," Sean said, casually swinging it open. Lawrence tensed, but no alarm blared in his ears. He followed Sean up the last short flight of steps and out onto the roof.

The cement was covered with gravel, dirt, cigarette butts and bird droppings. But Sean led him to where a waist-high cement wall surrounded the edge and swung out one arm as though he were personally responsible for the view.

It was beautiful. The city sprawled out, buildings catching the morning sunlight, the tops of the tallest ones still surrounded by mist. The breeze wafting through was cool and clean with an 'after rain' smell. Lawrence drew in a deep breath. "If they could figure out how to bottle that, someone would make a million dollars."

"Yeah, candles and laundry detergent never quite manage to capture it, do they?" Sean stood close, not quite touching him, but near enough that Lawrence could feel his warmth.

They watched the city moving and changing beneath them. "All those lives," Lawrence said. "All those people, each with their own thoughts, their own joys and sorrows."

Sean hummed in agreement. He slid closer, leaning against Lawrence, who put his arm around Sean. "People are going to want to study us, you know."

"Study us?"

"I don't think there's ever been a recorded case of two people in a relationship both successfully imbuing something or someone, especially within such a short span of time." He leaned against Lawrence. "Everyone's going to want to interview us, ask us about how it happened, study what we did..."

Lawrence shuddered. He never wanted to think about that moment again if he could help it. He would probably be seeing it in his nightmares for a long time as it was: the slide of the metal into Sean's flesh, the blood, the moment he realized what had happened —

"I'm all right," Sean said softly. Lawrence sucked in a breath he hadn't realized he'd been holding.

"Maybe we could..." he hesitated, swallowing.

"Could?"

"Maybe we could wait," Lawrence finished. "We could write down what happened and let people know someday but not — not yet. Maybe not until after we're gone."

Sean nodded, his head bobbing against Lawrence's shoulder. "That's a good idea."

"Okay. Good." Some of the tension flowed out of Lawrence's shoulders. "That's what we'll do, then."

~

It was a touch surreal, coming back to Sean's classroom the following Tuesday as though nothing had happened. Lawrence slipped in, the students ignored him, Sean gave him a quick, distracted smile and looked at the clock. "All right, that's all for today. Start cleaning your brushes, please. Are there any questions?"

Bobby once again raised a hand, barely waiting for Sean's nod before saying, "Isn't it true that imbuing can have multiple effects?"

Sean cocked his head to one side. "'Multiple effects'?" he echoed. "What do you mean?"

"Isn't it *true*," the student said, "that some people who've been healed by imbuing have been healed of more than one thing?"

Sean's eyes flicked to Lawrence for a long moment, then away. "Yes, that's true," he said slowly. "Sometimes people have been healed not only of an injury or illness, but also unrelated chronic issues."

Lawrence straightened, feeling his eyes go wide, his lips parting slightly. Had Sean...?

"Then," said Bobby doggedly, "doesn't that *prove* that—"

"It's not consistent," Sean cut him off. "Yes, there are a handful of cases where imbuing did more than just cure an immediate issue. However, there is a common thread in such cases: the person doing the imbuing had to *know* about the issues that were healed."

The breath caught in Lawrence's chest.

A flood of memories raced across his mind. All those small moments when Sean had seemed distracted or when he'd seemed like he wanted to tell Lawrence something. His expression when he'd gotten up in the morning. How energetic he'd been when they'd climbed the stairs to the roof.

Could Sean have been healed when Lawrence imbued him? Not just the wound, but the chronic issues that had caused him so much pain and difficulty for so long?

Trying not to get his hopes up, Lawrence watched Sean's face carefully. His own feelings wouldn't change no matter what the outcome had been, but if he'd been able to help Sean, if Sean didn't have to suffer so much anymore...hope bubbled up despite his best efforts, making his lungs feel huge and hollow.

The student looked frustrated. "It's God's *will!* Imbuing comes from Him, not from us."

"There are certainly many who believe that," Sean said smoothly. "But I'm afraid that's all the time we have. I will see you all on Thursday."

It probably didn't actually take an eon for the students to leave. Lawrence waited, trying not to show his impatience. When the last of them finally filed out, their chatting and laughter trailing behind them, he strode to the front of the room.

"Did I—" he started, meeting Sean's eyes. "Did you—?"

Sean gave him a single nod. "I think so. I haven't hurt since that afternoon. I didn't want to get my hopes up. I thought it might be psychosomatic. The placebo effect. But yesterday I didn't take my medication at all, and today I haven't felt a single twinge." He gave a shaky laugh. "I keep waiting for it, and it keeps not happening. It looks like you might have, maybe," he closed his eyes and pulled in a breath, "maybe cured me for good."

"Oh." Lawrence couldn't help reaching out. They'd agreed that they wouldn't do this at school, wouldn't give the students or their teachers unnecessary fodder for gossip or any chance to say that either of them had acted less than professionally. But Lawrence couldn't help it. He pulled Sean into his arms, and Sean went willingly, his cheek pressed to Lawrence's chest. "Sean," Lawrence murmured.

"I can't believe it," Sean said. "For so long I've had to endure it. And now, just like that, it's gone. The pain is gone." His voice dropped to a whisper. "Thank you."

"I didn't do anything," Lawrence said. "I didn't have any control over it. I would have chosen it if I could, but I wasn't given the option. It just happened."

"I know," Sean said. He tilted his face up, smiling when Lawrence leaned down to meet his lips with lingering, close-mouthed kisses that warmed Lawrence's blood. When they parted at last, Sean's face was flushed. "I want to paint you," he murmured. "I want to go to *all* of your matches. I want..." He trailed off and dropped his eyes, his smile widening again.

"Me too," Lawrence said. He wanted all of that, but mostly, "I want you," he said simply.

Sean's gaze darted up to his again, eyes going wide. He was alive and happy and in Lawrence's arms. That was all Lawrence really wanted.

"We're lucky," Lawrence whispered. "We're so lucky."

"Yeah," Sean said, his voice a little shaky. "I think we might be the luckiest people in the entire world."

Lawrence smiled back. "Yeah," he said. "I think you might be right."

About the Author

Janice L. Newman has come a long way from her college days as a music and Japanese major. A talented writer, she has contributed to *Rediscovery: Science Fiction by Women* and is currently working on more thrilling SFF romances. Janice's experience as a corporate controller makes her invaluable as the backbone for Journey Press and 3x Hugo Finalist Galactic Journey. She resides in San Diego with her writer husband, artist/writer/musician daughter, a gopher-eating cat, and a lump of a snake.

~

The lifeblood of every author is audience feedback. Please consider leaving a review (of whatever length) on Amazon, GoodReads, or your favorite platform.

About the Publisher

Founded in 2019 by Galactic Journey's Gideon Marcus, Journey Press publishes the best science fiction, current and classic, with an emphasis on the unusual, the diverse, and stories of hope.

Also available from Journey Press:

The magic is gone…or is it?

Lucian is a jaded flirt and professional bard who knows all the old songs about sorcery. When he meets Corwin, a shy mage who can still use magic despite the Drought, Lucian finds his desire growing with each passing day — not just for answers, but for Corwin himself.

**The Eighth Key
by Laura Weyr
A steamy fantasy romance**

One starship, six friends, 10,000 lives in the balance.

Young captain-for-hire Kitra Yilmaz has gotten her first contract: escort the mysterious Princess of Atlántida beyond the Frontier and find her a new world. It's a risky job, fraught with the threat of pirates, dangerous squatters, and rising romantic tensions.

**Sirena
by Gideon Marcus
Book 2 of the highly
acclaimed Kitra saga**